Duff got out. He hoisted the hood and stared at the engine, a black and brown jumble of hot greasy metal, totally different from the clean, intricate innards of a computer, and—to him—way more mysterious. A smell rose from it that scorched the inside of his nose.

I hate cars, he thought. Stupid Stone Age technology. He gave the front bumper a furious kick, and the right half of it came loose and fell across his foot.

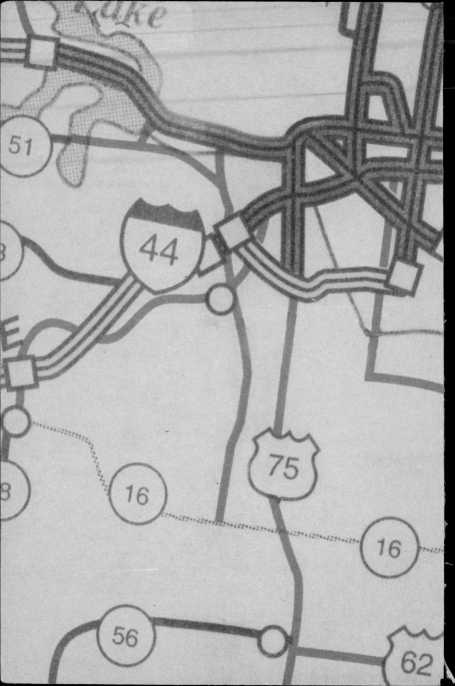

Jeanne DuPrau

CAR
TROUBLE

A NOVEL

A GREENWILLOW BOOK
HarperTempest®
An Imprint of HarperCollins Publishers

HarperTempest is an imprint of HarperCollins Publishers.

Car Trouble
Copyright © 2005 Jeanne DuPrau
All rights reserved. Printed in the United States of America. No part of this book may be used or reproduced in any manner whatsoever without written permission except in the case of brief quotations embodied in critical articles and reviews. For information address HarperCollins Children's Books, a division of HarperCollins Publishers, 1350 Avenue of the Americas, New York, NY 10019.

www.harperteen.com

Library of Congress Cataloging-in-Publication Data
DuPrau, Jeanne.
    Car Trouble / by Jeanne DuPrau.
       p.   cm.
    "Greenwillow Books."
    Summary: Early one August morning, seventeen-year-old computer "nerd" Duff Pringle leaves Richmond, Virginia, in a newly acquired used car and begins an unexpectedly convoluted journey to San Jose, California, and the job that awaits him there.
    ISBN-10: 0-06-073675-5 — ISBN-13: 978-0-06-073675-0
    [1. Travel—Fiction. 2. Automobiles—Fiction. 3. Interpersonal relations—Fiction. 4. Computers—Fiction.] I. Title.
PZ7.D927Car 2005   2004042467
[Fic]—dc22   CIP
                                                                    AC

Typography by Chad W. Beckerman
❖
First HarperTempest paperback edition, 2006

CONTENTS

1 DUFF DEPARTS 1

2 ON (AND OFF) THE ROAD 6

3 STUCK IN NOWHERE 22

4 THE GUY IN THE WILD SHIRT 38

5 THE COOL CAR 51

6 THE BIKERS' DANCE 69

7 THE CRIMINAL'S DEN 80

8 READY TO ROLL 97

9 AN ALL-NIGHT DRIVE 114

10 A STU PROBLEM 127

11 DUFF FALLS IN LOVE   143

12 STRANDED   158

13 AUNT SHIRLEY TO THE RESCUE   166

14 CRASHING AND SAVING   176

15 THE THIRD CAR   191

16 THE CHASE   211

17 TRUCK STOP   229

18 THE WEIRDNESS OF STU   238

19 SUNSET OVER THE OCEAN   254

20 A WHOLE DIFFERENT FUTURE   265

    The Last Chapter and
    THE LAST PHONE CALL   271

CAR

TROUBLE

Chapter 1
DUFF DEPARTS

He was ready. He stood on the front porch in the first light of dawn, with his duffel bag in one hand and in the other the carrying case that held his laptop computer. Out by the curb, his car awaited him—the small white Ford Escort he'd bought last week from Pete at the pizza place. It was a little banged up, but in the yellow glow of the streetlamp it looked better than in daylight. He took a long breath of warm, grassy-smelling air and ran the heading of his trip program through his mind: BEGIN: THE GREAT CROSS-COUNTRY JOURNEY OF DUFFY PRINGLE.

Behind him the screen door creaked open. His father came out, holding a cup of coffee wrapped in both hands. He stood beside Duff and gazed out at the car. "If you run into problems," he said, "you know what to do."

"I know," Duff said. "Call you right away."

"And when you get there, you know who to call if you need help."

"I know," Duff said. "Wade Belcher." Wade Belcher was some friend of his father's from a million years ago who now lived in San Jose. He was in the furniture business. Duff did not intend to call him.

"All right, then," his father said, nodding gloomily.

It was strange, Duff thought, not having to argue with him. For the last two weeks he'd argued nonstop with both parents: about how he ought to be going to college instead of to California, how he was too young to drive across the country alone, how there was probably some hitch to this job offer that sounded so good, and how he might know a lot about computers but he didn't know a thing about the real world and would probably wind up in jail or in the hospital or dead. "This isn't some computer program you can control by typing in a bunch of numbers," his father had said over and over. "This is *life*." He'd glare at him as if Duff had never heard of this advanced science called life and would never be able to master it.

But in the end, his parents didn't forbid him to go. They gave in, finally. They understood that their son, Duffy, had to be something special if a company on the other side of the country wanted to pay him good money to fool around with their computers.

Again the screen door opened. Duff's mother came out, rummaging through her purse for the name badge she wore at the restaurant. "Have you got your jacket, hon?" she said. "Did you pack some aspirin in case you get one of your headaches?"

Duff nodded. He'd forgotten actually. But he wasn't planning to have any headaches.

His mother stood on tiptoe and kissed his cheek. "Promise to drive real carefully, okay? Don't pick up any hitchhikers."

"You've got your cell phone?" his father asked.

"Naturally," Duff said.

"All right then," said his father. "If you run out of money, just call."

"I will," said Duff, though he knew he wouldn't. His father had no extra money. His business—Pringle Electric Works, Lamps & Lighting—never did much more than limp along. But Duff had the money he'd saved from working on weekends during his last year of high school; he was sure it would be enough for the trip.

He set down his bags and hugged his mom, who felt small and feathery in his arms. He hugged his dad, who felt large and stiff. Then he picked his bags up again and went down the steps to the street. His parents followed.

Duff opened the car door on the passenger side and laid his laptop on the seat, where it could ride next to him. The little computer was like a part of him—an external brain, a second pair of hands reaching out to the world. He put his duffel bag and a sleeping bag in the backseat. Then he got himself into the driver's seat and rolled down the window.

"Bye," he said to his parents, who had both bent slightly at the waist to look in at him.

"Call us from wherever you end up tonight," said his father.

"Don't forget," said his mother. "Bye, dear."

Duff turned the key in the ignition, and after a couple of coughs, the motor caught and hummed. He stepped on the gas and headed out into the street. It was so early that not a single other car was in sight.

Half a block on, he took one last look in the rearview mirror. His parents were still standing on the lawn, watching him go. He waved one more time, and they both waved back. Then he rounded a corner, they disappeared, and he was on his own, executing the first and most important line of his trip program: DRIVE WEST.

Chapter 2
ON (AND OFF) THE ROAD

He checked his watch. It was 6:03, Wednesday, June 26. He had six days to get from his hometown of Richmond, Virginia, to San Jose, California, which was approximately three thousand miles away. He would know *exactly* how many miles it was when he got there, because last night he had checked the car's odometer and noted the mileage in his trip log: 137,462.

Now he guided the car through the streets of his neighborhood. Good-bye, Happy Day Restaurant,

Art's Video Rental, Hoover Market, all these places he'd known forever. Good-bye and good riddance, Coolidge High School, home of airhead jocks, tyrant teachers, and girls with mean eyes and mocking laughs. He was no longer a citizen of this dreary place. He was heading out, bound for the open road.

He reached over and turned on the radio. Out came a blast of hideous noise, like a chain saw with sand in its engine. He punched the buttons and twirled the dial, but every single station sounded either like the chain saw or like fifteen people talking at once in foreign languages. Finally he gave up and turned the radio off. It wasn't really important. He'd brought along his CD player and his twelve favorite CDs. The kind of music he liked wasn't on the radio anyway.

The car seat seemed a little too far forward. He reached down and adjusted it. His legs had grown longer in the last year, turning him from a person of medium height to a truly tall person, almost tall enough to play basketball, if he had wanted to.

Ahead was the ramp leading onto the Beltway. Duff drove up and saw before him not the open road but a solid carpet of cars, three lanes wide, creeping forward at about five miles an hour. It was too early for rush hour traffic. There must be an accident up ahead. Duff wedged his car into the line. This was not what he'd had in mind. He'd pictured a clean, high-speed departure, like an arrow shot from a bow. He himself was the arrow, shooting from the grungy old city to the glittering towers of the high-tech world.

He loved the sound of that: the high-tech world. Everything would be different in San Jose, California, the heart of Silicon Valley, which (he'd been assured) was coming to life again after its recent downturn. His friends in San Jose would be people who talked about nanotechnology and artificial intelligence, not football scores and cars. He himself would be respected, finally. There would be no meatheads like Flynn Parker, who usually addressed Duff, when he spoke to him at all, as Loser Guy, and yelled, "Nerd attack! Take cover!" when he saw Duff coming into the cafeteria.

Duff didn't like the word *nerd*. He preferred *computer wizard*, *techie*, or even *geek*, all of which had an undertone of admiration that "nerd" lacked. He knew he appeared a little nerdlike—he couldn't help it, it was what happened when you spent long hours in a darkened room peering at tiny characters on a screen. In the past few years, he'd begun to look rather like a large, furry, burrowing animal—his hair was soft and brown and the same length all over his head, and he had a habit of hunching up his shoulders, stretching his neck forward, and squinting as if he were nearsighted. He had noticed this in his senior yearbook picture, and in the snapshots his father took at Christmas. But he didn't know what to do about it. Mostly, he didn't think much about his looks.

Traffic was still crawling. An endless line of winking brake lights stretched ahead. Duff inched forward, stopped, inched forward some more. He drummed his fingers on the steering wheel. Pretty soon, he felt Desperate Octopus Mind coming on.

This used to happen to him a lot in school. The

teacher would be droning on about something to do with laws or commas or exports of foreign countries, and there wouldn't be a single interesting word to latch on to. His mind would start thrashing around like an octopus, stretching its tentacles out in search of nourishment, and he'd end up calculating the number of tiles in the ceiling or silently reciting the alphabet backward or writing computer code on his arm.

Now he entertained himself by figuring out how many miles he'd traveled so far. The odometer registered 137,470. He'd gone 8 miles. It was 6:28. A quick mental calculation: he'd averaged about 16 miles per hour so far. Not good. At this rate, it would take him fifteen days to get to California, if he drove for twelve and a half hours a day.

With the tip of his finger, he wiped some gritty dust from the dashboard display. This car was not exactly in pristine shape—it was a dirty white, with four doors, ratty orange upholstery, and a couple of dents in the back bumper. But a local mechanic had taken a look at it and said it was all right. The only thing wrong with it was that the dashboard lights didn't work. That wasn't important, though. Duff wouldn't be doing much driving at night.

All he wanted was for this car to get him from the East Coast to the West. He wasn't interested in its insides. He knew that boys were supposed to be born with a gene that attracted them to car engines. But he was missing that gene—he was much more attracted to search engines. Lying in the grease under a two-thousand-pound hunk of metal, bending over the mess of rods and coils under the hood, spreading rusted motor chunks all over the driveway—none of this appealed to him at all.

The car had cost him $625, which left him $1,010 of the money he'd saved working weekends at Clyde's Computer Clinic. This seemed like a good number, for several reasons. It was composed of ones and zeroes, like machine language. *One* sounds like *won*, as in "I won!" And *one* means the beginning, which correlated with the beginning of his new life. Duff liked it when things worked out neatly like that. It was another reason he'd liked the amazing job offer—it came from a company called Incredibility, Inc., whose name began and ended with the same three letters.

In the months before he'd graduated from high school, Duff had put his resumé out on dozens of Internet job boards and sent customized letters to sixty-one companies that he thought he'd like to work for. Nothing much came of all this. But over the Memorial Day weekend, he'd gone to a conference in Baltimore—it was mostly about game programming—and met a guy there who put him in touch with a friend of his in San Jose. This friend—Ping Crocker was his name—was just starting a company to produce what he called "mind-boggling new products for the entertainment software market." His company was called Incredibility, Inc.

Duff looked up its website. It was flashy—brilliant colors, lots of animations, and sound effects including mad laughter and thunderous music. A little over-done, Duff thought, but definitely clever. He also did a search on "Ping Crocker" and "Incredibility, Inc."

He didn't find much, but he figured that was because the company was so new.

So he called Ping Crocker. Ping went on for twenty minutes about how Incredibility, Inc., was going to shape the future. They were ramping up for a project code-named "Rapid Vortex." It was a game-like product, Ping said, only it was way, way *more* than a game. It would blast open the whole *idea* of games, he said. Actually, it was more like a whole new *lifestyle* for the game-oriented person. For this project they desperately needed someone with skills that just happened to match the ones Duff had. He mentioned a very acceptable salary. Would Duff be interested?

Duff would.

Even his father had to admit it was pretty amazing for such a job to be offered to someone only seventeen years old. Still, he wanted Duff to turn it down and go to college instead. Duff felt fairly sure there was nothing at college he needed or wanted to learn. The whole idea of college made him nervous—a vast campus swarming with people, required classes in difficult but useless things like English and foreign languages, dorms full of athletes and possibly even girls. High school had been bad enough. He would learn on the job, he told his father.

Up ahead, Duff saw a cluster of flashing lights. He'd been right—it was an accident causing this slowdown. In a few minutes, he was creeping past it: two badly crumpled cars standing at odd angles on the side of the road. One of them had apparently caught fire; it was streaked with black, and dripping wet. Firemen and highway patrol officers were standing around with two forlorn-looking people, presumably the owners of the wrecked cars.

Like everyone else, Duff stared as he went by, felt glad it wasn't *his* accident, and drove on.

The traffic sped up right away. The speedometer needle was climbing toward thirty miles per hour. A few more miles and actual spaces opened up between the cars. Along the highway, Duff began to see green fields and trees. Soon he was going nearly fifty. This was more like it.

A stream of warm air rushed in the open window. The road was climbing up toward the hills. On both sides, dense woods made thick, billowy walls along the highway.

In San Jose, they had palm trees. He'd seen pictures of them on the Web. Living there would be like being on vacation in some tropical place all the time. He would find an apartment in a complex with a pool, and his salary would allow him to buy an even better computer system than he had now, plus any electronic gadget he wanted.

Ping Crocker had said he'd explain Project Rapid Vortex in detail after Duff arrived. Whatever this product was, Duff figured it would be a good start for a career that would eventually lead to great things. His goal was to invent something so spectacular that his name would start appearing in headlines: PRINGLE DEVELOPS NEXT-GENERATION SOMETHING-OR-OTHER! PRINGLE CALLED BOY WONDER OF 21ST CENTURY!

The truth was, Duff wanted to be important. He hadn't done any great things in his life so far, but somehow he knew he had the power to do them—he felt it within him, as strong as an oak sprout pushing up through concrete. Sometimes a sort of vision came to him: he saw himself immense, a giant standing astride the planet, one foot in New York, the other in Paris, a huge godlike figure to whom the citizens of the world looked up in awe. He wanted to do something that terrific. He didn't know yet exactly what it was, but he knew it had something to do with the vast, bright, speedy universe of electronics.

The face of his former classmate Flynn Parker rose before his eyes, smirking. He wished he'd had the chance (and the nerve) to have a little conversation with Flynn before they left school. He would have said, "What's next for you, Flynn? Gonna go work at Harvey's Burger Barn?"

"No," Flynn would say. "I've got a good job, geek-face. I'm working at the car wash."

"Great," Duff would say. "I'm going to California. Got a job in Silicon Valley."

Flynn would probably sneer in that way that

showed three teeth on the left side of his mouth and say, "Who cares, nerdbrain? I'd rather flip burgers than be as uncool as you."

"How much are you going to make at your job, Flynn?" Duff would politely inquire.

"None of your business," Flynn would say.

"Let me tell you what I'll be making," Duff would say, and he'd whisper the large figure of his monthly salary into Flynn's little red ear. Flynn's mouth would drop open and he'd look like a big dumb fish.

It was a satisfying scene.

In perfect contentment, Duff drove along Interstate 64 for the next three hours. His program was running smoothly. Ever since he'd planned this trip, he'd been thinking of it as a long computer program, composed mostly of the DRIVE command and direction indicators, and including subroutines that could be plugged in when needed, such as GET GAS, FIND PLACE TO EAT, and VIEW SCENIC SPOT. This was a habit he had, translating his life into a computer program. He didn't do it on purpose—it just happened, because

programming was so embedded in his way of thinking.
Arguments with his father, for instance, often resem-
bled infinite loops:

Dad: It's bad for you to sit at a computer screen
   all day.
Duff: Bad how?
Dad: Wrecks your eyesight.
Duff: My eyes are fine.
Dad: You need to get outside, play some basketball.
Duff: Why should I?
   [Back to the top.]

And if–then situations showed up all the time:

IF cafeteria lunch = spinach surprise
THEN buy sandwich from machine
ELSE go to cafeteria

Duff didn't see anything wrong with making his life
into a computer program. Thinking of it that way

made it seem more organized and manageable.

Around 9:30, somewhere in the green woodsy mountains close to West Virginia, just after he'd passed a road sign saying CHIPPER CROSSING, NEXT EXIT, the car started making a terrible noise. It was like the noise you hear when you drop a spoon down a garbage disposal: *grunk-grunk-grunnkk, ratcha-ratcha-grunk.* Duff whipped his foot off the accelerator. What was going on? The noise was so awful that he was afraid parts of the engine must be dropping onto the pavement and rolling away behind him. He veered into the slow lane, stepped hard on the brake, and came to a halt on the shoulder of the road. When the car stopped, the noise stopped, too.

Duff got out. He hoisted the hood and stared at the engine, a black and brown jumble of hot greasy metal, totally different from the clean, intricate innards of a computer, and—to him—way more mysterious. A smell rose from it that scorched the inside of his nose. Cars sped past on the highway, their drivers barely glancing at him, and the wind from their passing riffled the T-shirt he had bought especially for this trip, which said TWENTY TERAFLOP CAPABILITY across the front.

I hate cars, he thought. Stupid Stone Age technology. He gave the front bumper a furious kick, and the right half of it came loose and fell across his foot.

Phone Call #1

Wednesday, June 26, 9:37 AM

AAA recorded voice: You have reached
Triple A Road Service. Your call may be
monitored for quality assurance. To place a
new road service call, press 1.

Duff presses 1.

AAA recorded voice: Please hold. Your call
will be answered in the order it was received.

[Music—a sugary version of an ancient rock song]

Duff: Come on. Come on. Hurry up, hurry—

AAA real voice: Road service.

Duff: Oh, hi. My car has a problem.

AAA real voice: Your location?

Duff: Uh, 64. Just past the Chipper Crossing turnoff.

AAA real voice: And the problem?

Duff: Uh, engine noise. Pretty bad.

AAA real voice: Engine noise?

Duff: Yeah. And smell. Kind of a burning smell.

AAA real voice: Okeydoke. Be there in about thirty
minutes.

Chapter 3
STUCK IN NOWHERE

The tow truck arrived after about forty-five minutes. A guy with curly red hair got out and peered at Duff's engine. "Start her up for me," he said.

Duff turned the key, and the terrible noise shook the whole car.

"Hmm," said the tow truck man. "Sounds bad."

He hooked Duff's car to his tow truck, and the two of them drove off the highway to a gas station with a big garage in back. A man strolled out when he saw them coming. He was wearing an olive green shirt with

DAVE written on the pocket flap in orange script. His face was creased with lines that looked strangely dark—probably, Duff thought, because engine grease had settled into them.

Dave raised the hood of Duff's car and looked in.

"Well," he said after a while. "Looks to me like you have thrown a rod."

"Is that serious?"

"Yes, it is." Dave nodded slowly, looking quizzically at Duff, as if he'd never met anyone before who didn't understand what "thrown a rod" meant. Then he pointed down into the depths of the engine. "See that hole there?"

Duff saw it—a ragged hole in a piece of metal.

"That's where that rod shot through your engine."

"Oh, right," said Duff, nodding as if he understood. "How long will it take to fix?"

"Fix?" said Dave. "Well, you could order a new engine. Might take a week or so to get here. Might take a week to put it in. That's two weeks total, if you're lucky." Dave smacked the car's fender, which trembled. "Myself,

I wouldn't bother putting a new engine in this thing."

Duff leaned over the engine and stared into it, rubbing his chin, trying to look as if he were inspecting the damage. His mind felt strangely blank and still, except for the words *two weeks* and *wouldn't bother*, which hung in the blankness like neon signs. He waited for ideas. He drummed his fingers on the fender. He stalled for time.

"What do you think went wrong for this car to throw a rod?" he said.

Dave leaned against the passenger door and crossed his arms over his chest. "Did you maybe see the oil light flashing just before it happened?"

"No," Duff said.

"Huh," said Dave. "Don't know how you could have missed it."

With a sinking feeling, Duff realized that not having dashboard lights was more of a problem than he'd thought. He decided not to mention this.

"The point is," said Dave patiently, "you didn't get oil in there in time, and now your engine is shot."

"I have to think about this," said Duff. "Can I leave the car here for a while?"

"Sure."

Duff fetched his laptop from the car and slung the strap of its carrying case over his shoulder. He set off down the road in what looked to be the direction of town. It was mortifying, being stuck on the first day of his journey. But he knew already what he wasn't going to do: (1) call his parents to come and rescue him, (2) sit around for two weeks waiting for a new engine, (3) spend a big chunk of his money on a plane ticket to California. He had his heart set on driving across the country, and somehow he was going to do it.

When the job offer first came, he'd assumed he'd be flying to California. They wanted him to start the new job on July first, which was about three weeks away. But as soon as he accepted the job, a huge restlessness gripped him. Everything around him suddenly looked unbearably gray and dreary, his own house especially, with its musty old curtains that kept the living room in twilight, and the cracked linoleum in the kitchen, and the narrow hallway where he was always bumping into his father or his mother now that he'd gotten so big. He could hardly stand the thought of waiting three more weeks to get on a plane and fly away.

One night as he was roaming around on the Web, he came across a site called ScenicAmerica.com. As he looked at the pictures of the St. Louis arch and the Grand Canyon and Death Valley, thinking about how he'd never seen anyplace more distant than Ocean City, where his grandparents lived, and the inside of a hotel in Baltimore, where he'd gone that time for the computer conference, it suddenly occurred to him that all these famous American sights were *on the way* to California. Why fly twenty thousand feet above them and see them as dots when he could drive across the country and see them close up? Best of all: if he drove, he could leave right away. Well, almost right away, as soon as he could find himself a car.

He made up his mind to do it. And when Duff made up his mind about something, he threw himself into it. That's how he'd always been, from the time he wrote an entire twenty-six-page novel about space aliens at the age of eight, to the time he discovered computers at the age of eleven. Now he threw himself into planning his trip. He traced his route on Internet road map sites, figuring out where he would stop each night. He set up a spreadsheet to budget his expenses. He made a list of all the sights he wanted to see on the way.

When he had his trip planned out, he printed the pages and put them in a binder with a label on the front that said merely TRIP. Actually, he thought of it as The Great Cross-Country Journey of Duffy Pringle, though he wasn't going to write that where anyone could see it. He pictured this journey as a marker between his rotten old life and his wonderful new life. He would leave childhood behind and arrive at adulthood (truly, because he'd be eighteen on the third of July), and on the way he'd see America.

What he was seeing of America right now, though, was not especially scenic. There was no sidewalk along the road toward town. Big rangy shrubs and weeds grew beside the gravel verge of the pavement, with various kinds of litter—flattened paper cups, straw wrappers, magazine pages—caught in their leaves. Farther on, he passed a two-story brick building whose sign said DOZE INN, VACANCY, and beyond that another road turned off to the left and became, after a short distance, a street lined with stores. This had to be downtown Chipper Crossing.

It looked to Duff like a place that hadn't even caught up with the twentieth century, let alone the twenty-first. There was one intersection busy enough to have a stoplight, which swung on a low wire stretched across the street. Two cars and a bicycle were waiting for the green. Duff passed a department store window where boy and girl mannequins with smiling, grayish faces and little mittenlike hands modeled summer clothes. In a coffee shop, he saw a few people sitting at a row of stools at a counter. The smell of doughnuts drifted through the door. There was a dry cleaners, a variety store, a shoe store, a drugstore (that one breathed out a smell of cherry cough drops), but Duff saw no sign of what he was looking for—a place to connect his laptop to the Internet. He knew his wireless interface wouldn't work—hot spots were only in cities, not in places like this.

He almost walked right past the Chipper Crossing Public Library. It didn't look like a library. It looked like a dentist's office, with a door that had a glass panel in its top half, printed with gold-edged letters. He was in luck. The library was open only three hours a day, and right now was one of them. They had to have a computer in there, didn't they, with an Internet connection?

Inside was a room lined with bookshelves. A roundish woman with short, straight hair and rimless glasses sat at a desk at the far end, flanked by tall circular racks of paperbacks. She was the only person in the room. She looked up when he came in, gave him a smile, and went back to the book she was reading.

Duff looked around. He saw no computers. Behind

the librarian was a wooden file cabinet with four brass-handled drawers labeled with letters of the alphabet. This was a bad sign.

"Excuse me," he said to the librarian. "I need to connect to the Web."

The librarian looked up. She smiled at him again, rather blankly, as if her mind were elsewhere, and closed her book, which was titled *Murder at the Five and Dime*. "The Web," she said. "Oh, yes, the Web. Right! We don't have that here."

"The Web is everywhere," said Duff.

"Well, but not here. Not yet! We'll have it soon! But right now, only our main county branch is connected."

"Where's that?" Duff asked.

"Just over at Martinsville," she said, pointing out the window.

"How far away is it?"

"Oh, twenty miles or so," she said cheerfully. "It's quite a lovely library. Anything else I could help you with? Any books you're looking for?"

Yeah, thought Duff, how about *The Complete Book*

of Car Engines and How Not to Wreck Them? But he only shook his head, said, "Thanks anyway," and left.

He walked back down the other side of Main Street. The strap of his carrying case was digging a groove in his shoulder, and sweat was making his T-shirt stick to his back. He passed the coffee shop again. Warm, sugary smells were still wafting through the door, so he went in and bought a jelly doughnut to help him think. How was he going to solve this transportation problem if he couldn't get on to the Internet? The Internet was his all-purpose problem solver. There was no one he could call on the telephone—the friends he knew best were e-mail friends, and he didn't even have their phone numbers. He could think of only one solution: he was going to have to find a motel room right now, even though it was only nine-thirty in the morning, and plug his laptop into a phone line. It was even possible that he'd need a motel room for sleeping in, if he couldn't find a way to get out of here by nighttime.

So he trudged back to the motel he'd seen out at

the edge of town—the Doze Inn. In the office, a sour-faced woman stood behind the counter. She wore a badge that said, WELCOME! I'M MRS. EDNA FOOTE. There was a smiley face on the badge, which must have made Mrs. Foote feel that she didn't have to smile herself. Duff filled out a form, and Edna Foote handed over the key to room 26. She didn't ask if he was old enough to rent a motel room. Duff didn't expect she would. Something about his height, his slightly stooped posture, and his serious expression made people think he was older than he was.

Inside room 26, there was a large hard bed, a wooden desk, and a big painting on the wall of some cowboys riding over a grassy plain. Duff had never been in a motel room by himself before. It made him feel a little lonely. He opened the window and looked out at the view. Across the road were some scraggly trees, and beyond them was the highway, where cars and trucks roared past. The odor of exhaust floated up to him. He thought of all the rods in all those cars, doing whatever rods were supposed to do, and how for want of a few drops of oil those rods would run amok and shoot the engines to death. It seemed like a bad system.

And it wasn't just cars that needed oil, but pretty much the whole country. People were constantly arguing about where the oil was going to come from. Should we suck it up out of some remote wilderness? Should we drill for it in the ocean? Other countries had plenty of oil down underneath their deserts, but we could only get at it if we stayed friends with them (even though they were sometimes run by dictators or harbored terrorists) or went to war with them. It seemed to Duff that the whole oil thing was a major pain in the neck.

He turned away from the window. All right, he told himself, focus on the problem. He took off his shoes and lay down on the bed to do some preliminary thinking. Clearly, he needed a new car. Just as clearly, he couldn't afford to buy one. He had $200 in cash in his wallet—no, $150 now that he'd paid for the motel room—and $810 in a checking account that he could access with his bank card. Any decent car would cost more than he'd paid for this one, which would leave him without enough money: he not only had to buy gas and food for the trip, he had to have enough left for the first month's rent on an apartment. He refused to call his parents for help. So what options did that leave? Take the bus to California? A depressing thought.

Duff took some deep breaths of the room's stale air to get more oxygen into his blood and bicycle-pedaled his legs to get more blood flowing to his brain. Finally, after a period of blankness, one long-shot idea floated into his mind. It was worth a try.

He went to the desk, plugged his laptop into the telephone jack, and logged on to the Internet. He roamed about, checking message boards. It took him a while, but eventually he found this ad:

DRIVER WANTED

NEED SOMEONE TO DRIVE CAR

FROM LEXINGTON VA TO ST. LOUIS MO ASAP.

CARL H.

Duff rattled off an answer:

Carl—
I cd drive yr car to St. Louis. I'm in Chipper Crossing,
VA. Pls contact me ASAP.
Thx.
Duff Pringle

After that, there was nothing to do but wait. Duff occupied himself by Googling "internal combustion engine" and reading up on everything he should have known before. He hadn't actually realized that *explosions* made cars go. Gas and spark coming together, blam blam blam, hundreds of times a minute! An engine was nothing but a kind of controlled bomb. No wonder it was likely to blow up.

After a while, when there was still no reply from Carl, Duff got too restless to sit around the motel room. He walked back down to the gas station, where Dave greeted him cheerfully and asked if he'd decided what to do. "I'm working on it," Duff said. "I'll have it figured out pretty soon." His car was sitting off by itself with its hood up. Somehow it already looked like a piece of abandoned junk.

He walked back to the motel very slowly, trying to give Carl plenty of time to find his message and answer it. Sure enough, a reply was waiting for him:

Great. Yr only 20 miles away. Who are u?

Duff wrote back:

On my way to CA to start job in Silicon Valley. Car broke down. Need wheels ASAP. Can u bring car here?

Right away, he got this answer:

OK!!!!!! Tell me where.

After three more exchanges, they'd agreed: Carl would have the car there by one o'clock. Duff would drive it to St. Louis, arriving some time that night. He'd get paid $50, on arrival, for his trouble.

Duff felt so good about this ingenious solution to his problem that he did a little power dance around the motel room, stamping his bare feet on the dust-colored carpet and punching his fists in the air. Who says he knows nothing but computers? Who says he can't make it in the real world?

Chapter 4
THE GUY IN THE WILD SHIRT

It was only eleven o'clock. He had two hours before Carl came with the car. The first thing he did was walk back to the gas station and sell his dead Ford for $200 to Dave, who would use it for parts. That gave him $350 in his pocket in addition to the $810 in his checking account.

Another guy was at the station along with Dave this time—a young guy with long, stringy hair who was crouched down beside the wheel of a jacked-up car. He seemed to be working on the car, though he didn't look much like a mechanic. He had on a wild shirt printed with tropical birds in blazing red, yellow, orange, and purple. He wore a little gold loop in one ear. He had on shorts that showed his pale, hairy legs, and on his feet were sandals with complicated black straps. Maybe that was his own car he was working on. Maybe he'd had a breakdown, too.

Duff went back to the motel room and took a brief nap, since he was probably going to be driving most of the night. When he woke up, he was hungry. The jelly doughnut had worn off. So he locked his door and headed toward downtown.

He walked with a springy step down the gravel shoulder of the road. Whenever he came to a smashed paper cup or a burger wrapper or someone's old sock, he kicked it back under the bushes so the road wouldn't look so trashy. He almost wished his father were with him, so he could tell him that his computer know-how had just solved a major real-life problem. His father was always saying he shouldn't be so focused on one thing. "When you get out in the real world," he said, "you'll fall on your face. You gotta start thinking about something besides computers."

Well, so far, for a total geek, he was doing just fine. Besides, it wasn't true that he never thought about anything but computers. Sometimes he thought about his social life, or rather his lack of it. He thought about his future, which would involve lots of money and some sort of electronic greatness. Now and then he even thought about the state of the world, when he happened to see a newspaper headline or watch a special on TV. He knew the air was polluted, the ice caps were melting, the rain forests were being chopped down, the fish were croaking in the poisoned lakes, and the sea birds were mucked up by oil spills. There were wars all over the place, because Country 1 wanted what Country 2 had, and Country 3 wanted what Country 1 had, and Country 4 didn't have anything. He knew about all that. But he didn't dwell on it. Why should he? There was nothing he could do about it.

The coffee shop was full of people. All the stools

at the counter were occupied, and so were the three spindly tables near the window. At one of these tables, he saw the guy who'd been at the gas station an hour or so ago—the one with the tropical shirt. The guy noticed Duff, too. He pointed his fork at him and said, "Hey. Seen you at Dave's."

Duff nodded.

"Have a seat," said the guy, giving a shove with his foot to the empty chair at his table.

"Thanks," said Duff. He sat down.

"You live here?" said the guy. He had big rabbity front teeth, and his blondish hair fell in wiggly strands down the back of his neck.

"No," said Duff. "I'm here because my car broke down."

"Oh, bummer," said the guy. "So it's being fixed?"

"Nope," said Duff. "Can't be fixed."

"Whoa," said the guy. "What are you going to do?"

"I have a plan," said Duff. He was proud of his plan, and tempted to talk about it—but he didn't know this person, so he hesitated.

The guy held out his hand, as if he could tell what Duff was thinking. "I'm Stu," he said. "Stu Sturvich. I'm heading for California."

Duff shook his hand and introduced himself. "You're driving?"

"No, hitching," said Stu. "But man, it's hard to get a ride around here. I stood out there by the freeway entrance for hours this morning. People just looked at me and drove on. Finally I gave up. Went and found that garage and hired myself out to the guy there for a few hours."

"You're a mechanic?"

"Oh, yeah. Not a pro, but I know everything about cars. Cars are my thing."

"But you don't have one," Duff noted.

"Well, not right now," Stu said. He didn't explain further.

A waitress in a pink outfit came by, and Duff ordered a grilled cheese sandwich, fries, a strawberry milkshake, and two pieces of apple pie.

"So why are you going to California?" he asked Stu.

"To surf, for one thing," said Stu. He stood up abruptly from the table, flung his arms out, bent his knees, and assumed a twisted-sideways position. "Hang ten, man," he said. "Wipeout." He grinned. There was ketchup on his big front teeth. Then he sat down again and said, "Are you going that direction?"

Duff nodded.

"Getting yourself a new car?" Stu asked.

"Driving one for someone else."

"Any chance I could get a ride with you? Even part way?"

Duff hesitated.

"Share expenses?" said Stu. "I have some cash."

Ordinarily, Duff would have said no right away to such an offer. But he was in a good mood just then because he'd solved his transportation problem. And Stu seemed a friendly kind of guy, easygoing, laid-back. Duff wasn't used to easy, friendly, laid-back people. His friends, the few he had, were mostly very much like himself, more on the tense, serious side. It might be refreshing to know someone like Stu, he thought. But was Stu only being friendly because he wanted a ride?

It occurred to him that he could find this out by running a little test.

"Here's the problem," he said. "This car I'm getting—I'm like ninety percent sure the owner wouldn't want me to take a hitchhiker along. So . . ." He held out his hands, palms up. "Sorry, but I think I better not offer you a ride."

Stu's face fell. "Really?" he said. "You sure? I wouldn't get the seats dirty or anything."

"I better not," said Duff.

Stu sighed. He took a big bite of his hamburger and chewed on it for a while, staring down at his plate. "Well," he said, "thanks anyway. I'll just get out the old thumb again. Want this pickle? I don't do pickles."

"Sure," said Duff. He stuck the pickle into what was left of his cheese sandwich.

"What's that mean on your T-shirt?" Stu asked.

Duff looked down at his chest, forgetting what his T-shirt said. Oh, yeah: TWENTY TERAFLOP CAPABILITY.

"It's the speed of a superfast computer," he said. "A teraflop is a trillion floating-point operations per second. Like, you know, doing a trillion math problems in one second."

"Wow," said Stu. "So you're into techie stuff? That's so cool. I never learned any of that in my lousy school. One ancient Apple in each class that nobody knew how to use. Might as well have been 1960 in that dump. The pencil sharpener didn't even work."

"Where'd you go to school?"

"Florida. It was this little town no one has ever heard of." He slurped the last of his soda, making a gargling noise with his straw. "So say something in high tech," he said. "I like to hear it."

Duff thought for a second. Then he rattled off a long sentence—it didn't make much sense, but Stu would never know—containing the words gigahertz, hexadecimal, turbocharged hard drive, nanotechnology, and spherical harmonic functions.

"Man, that is awesome," said Stu. "I don't know what a single one of those words means." He balled up his paper napkin and lobbed it toward the wastebasket across the room. It missed, but he didn't seem to care. "I guess you can make a bundle doing high-tech work, can't you," he said.

"Oh, yeah," said Duff. "I'm planning to, for sure."

"I'd like the money," Stu said, "but I wouldn't like the work. It's amazing to me, you guys who can do that stuff. I guess geeks kind of run the world now."

Duff smiled modestly. This had never happened to him before—to have someone be actually interested in what he knew, and even impressed by it. And Stu couldn't be just buttering him up, because Duff had already said he wasn't giving him a ride. This must be a genuine kind of guy, an unprejudiced, open-minded guy, with at least half a brain.

By the time they'd finished eating, and Stu had expressed his admiration for Duff's knowledge several times, Duff had started to think, Why *not* have this guy along for the ride? In his mind, he set up a chart to examine the question. On one side were the pluses, on the other the minuses.

On the plus side: Stu was willing to share expenses, and he had some money. He knew about cars, which could come in handy. He seemed pretty friendly, not the jock type, although Duff guessed surfing was a kind of jockism. But at least it didn't involve shoving other guys over or trampling their faces into the dirt.

On the minus side: He hadn't pictured making this trip with another person, someone he'd have to talk to. Duff had a hard time with conversation. Words didn't just spring out of him the way they did from some people. He had to find them in his head and put them together. Even after he'd done this, they often came out wrong. He couldn't see it, but other people did. He could tell from the way they pressed their lips together trying not to laugh and looked sidelong at one another. Why talk to people at all if they were going to be like that? But the more he didn't talk to people, the harder it was when he *did* talk to people, because he never got any practice. Maybe he could get some practice with Stu.

On the whole, it seemed like the plus side outweighed the minus. At least I could take him as far as St. Louis, Duff thought. I'll tell him I'm only going that far, and then if I don't like traveling with him I can ditch him there.

"I wish I *could* give you a ride," he said as they left the coffee shop. "Hold on—let me try something." He got out his cell phone and punched in the number for getting the correct time.

"The time . . . ," said the operator, "is . . ."

"Hi," Duff said into the phone. "This is Duff, the one who's going to drive your car?" He paused.

"And forty seconds," said the operator.

"Yeah," Duff said. "I wanted to ask you a question. Would it be okay with you if I brought along a friend to share the driving?" He paused again, listening to the time lady say, "At the tone, the time will be . . ."

Then he said, in a surprised voice, "Really? That's great. Thanks a lot!" and pressed the Off button.

"It's okay?" said Stu. It was sort of touching, how pleased he looked. His eyebrows went way up, and his eyes got round.

"Yeah," said Duff. "They don't mind. I'm taking the car to St. Louis, so I can drive you that far."

"Oh, thanks!" Stu clapped Duff on the arm. "This is fantastic. Thanks a lot!"

"The guy's bringing the car to that motel out by the gas station. Meet me there about one-thirty." He wanted Stu to arrive after Carl had safely left, just in case the real-life Carl didn't want him to take a passenger.

Stu grinned. "Thanks, dude," he said. "I really appreciate it. This is going to be great."

In his mind, Duff heard the faraway echo of his mother's voice saying, "Don't pick up any hitchhikers." He'd forgotten to add that to the minus side of the chart. But it wasn't important. It was just something people said, like "Don't talk to strangers." He felt pleased with himself, in fact, for not being chained to an archaic parental rule. An independent person had to judge each situation separately. He was going to trust his intuition on this one.

Chapter 5
THE COOL CAR

At one o'clock, Duff was in the Doze Inn's parking lot sitting on his duffel bag. At one ten, a car pulled in.

It was a huge car. Its long, streamlined body projected way out in front and way out in back. Chrome-edged tail fins pointed backward on either side of the trunk, like the fins of twin sharks. The car made a slow turn into the motel parking lot from the street, scraping its low front end on the pavement. It pulled up in front of Duff and stopped. Just behind it was a green compact, which also stopped.

The window of the big car went down, and the driver poked his head through and said, "You Duff Pringle?"

"Correct," Duff said. "You're Carl?"

"Right." The car door opened, and a scrawny guy in a black T-shirt got out. He looked about Duff's age, maybe a year or two older. At first Duff thought he had a smudge of engine grease or maybe chocolate milk just below his nose. Then he realized it was a thin mustache.

Carl stuck out a hand. "Carl Hopgood," he said, "and that back there is my girlfriend, Angie." He pointed at the small green car. Inside, Duff could see a girl with a reddish black pony tail and very long eyelashes. She opened the window and waggled her fingers at him, then got out and walked over to Carl. He wound one of his long arms around her waist, and she curved herself against him.

Carl smiled and gave her ponytail a tug. "I'm ridin' back with her," he said. "See, this aunt of mine wanted me to drive her car to St. Louis tonight, and I said okay, because she was going to give me fifty bucks for doing it, but then Angie told me about this party a guy is having over where we live. It's one of those parties you don't want to miss, know what I mean?" Carl sniggered and bumped his hip against Angie's. Angie bumped him back and draped an arm across his shoulders. "So I thought, hey, maybe I can get someone else to drive the thing for me. And I got lucky!"

"Yeah," said Duff. "Me, too. What kind of car is this, anyway?"

"Oh, it's a classic. Chevrolet Bel Air, 1957."

"Nineteen fifty-seven?" Duff did a fast calculation. "You mean this car's, like, half a century old?"

"Yep. Works pretty good, too. Rosalie, that's my aunt, she bought it from one of those car fanatics. She's gonna get it totally renovated." Carl reached into the front seat and retrieved a piece of paper. "Here's the directions to her house in St. Louis. She wants the car there by tonight, she said. You better be there. My aunt Rosalie is not one to mess with, I'll tell you that, because she—"

Angie tweaked Carl's ear. He yelped. "You're just

talking and talking, honey," Angie said to him.

Carl pouted. In a babyish voice, he said, "That hurt."

"I'll make it better," said Angie. She kissed Carl's ear, and he grinned.

Duff wondered how anyone could like having his ear kissed. "Did you tell your aunt you're getting someone else to deliver the car?" he asked Carl.

" 'Course not," Carl said. "Why should I? She'd just get all upset. Only thing that matters is the car gets there. She doesn't have to know who's driving it." He narrowed his eyes and glared at Duff. "You *will* get it there, right? 'Cause if you don't, I'll have to tell her it got stolen from me by a hitchhiker I picked up named Duff Pringle."

Duff frowned. He didn't like this guy. He didn't like the girlfriend, either, whose pale little eyes peered out at him from under those spidery eyelashes. But he needed the car. "I'll get it there," he said. "Will your aunt be there for me to deliver it to?"

"Nope," said Carl. "Somebody will. Probably my cousin. I'll call and say you're coming." He tossed the car keys to Duff. "Here you go. Have a good trip."

Carl and Angie, their fingers hooked in each other's belts, walked away toward the small green car. Carl murmured something; Angie giggled and gave him a shove. Carl reached for her ponytail; she dodged away from him. They got in the car still laughing and roared away.

A sleazeball, thought Duff. Both of them were sleazeballs. He hated that kind of mushy behavior; it made his skin crawl. If, some day in the remote future, he decided he wanted a girlfriend, he would have to find one who did not giggle and who would never kiss his ear.

He turned his attention to the amazing car. But before he'd had a chance to examine it, he saw Stu trudging into the parking lot, a backpack on his back. When Stu saw the car, he started trotting toward it.

"Is this it, man? The car we're driving?"

"This is it," said Duff.

"You have got to be kidding," said Stu. He shrugged off his backpack and let it fall to the pavement. He stood staring at the car with his mouth open for a moment, and then he began circling it slowly, like an animal sniffing. He ran his fingers over the chrome V in the front, and over the two hood ornaments, and across the grill, which looked to Duff like the evil grin of someone with a lot of braces.

"Man," Stu breathed, "I've never been this close to one of these."

"What's so great about it?" Duff said.

"Just one of the coolest cars ever made," said Stu. "Too bad no one's been taking care of it. Looks a little banged up." He unlatched the hood and peered inside. "Engine's not real clean," he said. "Man, I'd sure love to get my hands on this car. All fixed up, it could be worth twenty thousand dollars. Or even more."

Duff felt a twinge of nervousness. He'd have to watch for flashing lights on the dashboard. Stop at the first hint of a funny noise. He could sense that damaging Rosalie Hopgood's property—which was going to be worth a lot some day but wasn't yet— would not be a good idea.

"Let's get going," Duff said. "We're supposed to be there by tonight."

They loaded their things into the car's enormous trunk. When Duff sat down behind the wheel, he felt small. The hood of the car extended into the distance in front of him, vast and level as a plain.

He examined the dashboard. "We're going to have to watch the oil light carefully," he said with a knowledgeable air. "An old car like this, it might have a tendency to run out of oil."

He started the car and moved it slowly through the parking lot and into the street. It was like maneuvering an aircraft carrier. What was the back end doing? Was it following along? Was it about to hit something?

Once they got onto the highway, he calmed down. The car did run smoothly. It glided. Being encased in that much metal and glass made him feel safe. Beside this one, other cars on the road looked like little tin bubbles.

Stu sprawled happily in his seat. He turned up the radio, which was tuned to an oldies station currently playing "Hound Dog," by Elvis Presley. "This is cool," he said. "Look how people are staring at us."

It was true. The car turned heads. It was a new sensation for Duff, who had never before attracted attention for being cool.

They glided along through the green hills of West Virginia. Duff kept glancing at the oil light, but it didn't blink once. The radio played "(I Can't Get No) Satisfaction," "Blueberry Hill," and "Sergeant Pepper's Lonely Hearts Club Band." Warm air blew through the open windows and whipped Stu's stringy strands of hair against his face. Duff breathed a long, contented breath.

He breathed again, this time sniffing the air. "Do you smell something?" he asked Stu.

Stu sniffed, too. He wrinkled his nose. "Exhaust," he said. "Maybe we should put the windows back up."

"Is it us or someone else?" Duff asked.

His question was answered a second later, when a red Toyota passed and its driver glared at them and held his nose as he went by. Duff looked in the rearview mirror and saw a cloud of thin gray smoke. "Yuck," he said.

"Old engines," said Stu. "They don't burn clean."

"But that doesn't mean we're going to break down or anything," said Duff.

"No, no. Just a little stink." Stu propped his feet on the dashboard. His knees stuck up in front of his face, which was halfway down the seat. He said, "So what do you do with yourself, Mr. Duffy, when you're not out driving?"

"I work on my projects, mostly."

"On your computer?"

"Correct."

"Like what would a typical project be?"

"Well, right now I'm working on a virus detector for incoming e-mail files, and also a really good RAM optimizer."

"Uh-huh," said Stu. "So that's what you do *all the time*? Morning, afternoon, and night?"

"Pretty much. This stuff is nontrivial. You have to know a lot."

"Yeah, but don't you get restless, man? Sitting in the same old room all day, staring at that same old screen? Don't you want to have some fun ever?"

"My projects *are* fun, to me," Duff said. "I've designed some games, too. Spitballs from Hell is my best one." He felt a surge of pleasure just thinking about that awesome game. "I designed a slick interface for it," he said, "and I got it to go incredibly fast by using this algorithm I developed pretty much on my own. And the graphics weren't even too shabby, considering I'm not exactly an artist." Duff grinned, remembering how clever he'd been. "See, the game has eleven levels," he said, and he would have gone on to explain the whole thing if he hadn't glanced over at Stu and seen him shaking his head in a slow and mystified way.

"Whatever turns you on," Stu said. "See, what you like and what I like aren't the same. What I like is to find a girl who knows how to have a good time, and then we take the boom box down to the beach and have a picnic. Or we go dancing. A girl who laughs a lot, that's the kind I like."

Not me, thought Duff, remembering April Parmalee back in high school, a big laugher. She liked to make other people laugh, too. She often got good laughs by talking in a goofy, hooting way that was supposed to be an imitation of Duff. Very funny.

Stu turned toward Duff, hooking his elbow over the seat back. "You have a girlfriend, man?"

"No," said Duff shortly. He felt wounded by Stu's lack of interest in his game. "I don't really have time for girls."

"Because you work on your computer all the time?"

"Most of the time."

"But how come the girls aren't after *you*, man? You're a big tall guy, they like that. You'd be good-looking if you did something different to your hair. And if you didn't look so freakin' serious."

"I can't help looking serious," said Duff. "I *am* serious. I am just not interested in wasting my time doing pointless stuff like sitting on the beach with some girl."

"Maybe you're gay," said Stu.

"No," said Duff. "I am not."

"Some people are and don't know it," said Stu.

Duff had never understood how people could not know what sex they were attracted to. It was just there inside you, a magnetic pull. He had felt it, strongly, twice: for Melissa Nimberger in eighth grade, and for Megan Bent his junior year. He'd never felt it for a boy, but he imagined that kids who had would know it perfectly well. How could you not?

"I'm trying to tell you," he said to Stu. "It's not that I don't like girls, I just don't have time for them right now." He knew of course that this wasn't true. If, for instance, Megan Bent had knocked on the door of his parents' house some night and asked to see him, he would have leaped up from his important project and wasted as many hours with her as she wanted. The problem wasn't that he didn't like girls, it was that girls didn't like him. Or didn't notice him. Or noticed him in the wrong way.

Stu appeared to lose interest in the conversation after that. He took a couple of sticks of gum out of his pocket, unwrapped them, and threw the wrappers out the window. "Gum?" he said to Duff.

"No, thanks." Duff didn't go for littering. Why mess up the highway even more than it was messed up already, with billboards and abandoned tires and squashed animals? But he didn't say this to Stu. He didn't feel like talking to Stu at the moment.

Stu chewed for a while, gazing out the window, and then his head gradually tilted sideways until it was resting against the glass, and he went to sleep. His mouth dropped open, showing the wad of gum stuck to a lower tooth. Occasionally his leg twitched, and he made little muttering sounds.

Duff drove, brooding about his social life. It was as if he had an unresolved bug in his personality program, a bad line of code that caused him, whenever a girl spoke to him, to split into two people. One was The Speaker, who said something in reply to the girl, and the other was The Listener, who told him how asinine what he had just said was and suggested several other things that would have been better. This had been going on for years. He was afraid he was doomed to be chewed out by The Listener for the rest of his life, which would mean he would never have a normal conversation with a girl, because he would be too distracted by The Listener's constant criticism.

He brought his thoughts back to the present. Better check those dashboard gauges and make sure everything was all right. Nothing was flashing. But the needle of the gas gauge was pointing almost directly to the "E." How could they have used up a whole tank of gas already? Of course, maybe Carl hadn't started them out with a full tank. He'd forgotten to check.

Duff poked Stu, who woke up with a start. "We're stopping for gas," Duff said. He took the next exit and found a gas station. A cheerful-looking man wearing a blue shirt with PHIL embroidered on the pocket flap watched as they drove in. He looked over the car admiringly. "This is a nice old baby," he said. "You've definitely got a problem with your emissions, though. Your exhaust is spewing out a good number of noxious chemicals."

"Oh," said Duff. "Like what?"

"Oh, stuff like carbon monoxide. That's the one

people pump into the car when they want to commit suicide. Also hydrocarbons that tend to wreck the atmosphere of the planet. Little problems like that."

"Can you fix it?"

"Well, I'd have to take the engine apart to see why it isn't burning clean. Probably take me at least two or three days."

"That's no good," said Duff. "We have to be in St. Louis by tonight."

Phil shrugged and grinned and held his hands out sideways, palms up. "Can't help you, then," he said.

They filled up the tank. Duff watched the numbers scroll by on the gas pump. "How many miles per gallon does a car like this get?" he asked Phil.

"Oh, these old cars get maybe twelve or fourteen miles a gallon," said Phil.

"Not too good," said Duff.

"Yep. It's terrible. Your newer cars, now, especially those hybrids, they can get forty or fifty or even more. Except for the big SUVs, of course, which don't do much better than this old thing."

Duff did a quick mental calculation. Every twelve miles he'd be paying for a gallon of gas. Between here and San Jose was something like 2500 miles. Divide 12 into that, multiply by the price of gas—Duff let out a quiet whistle. It was a significant sum.

"So why would anyone these days want to drive a car like this?" he asked. "And pay two or three times as much for gas?"

"Because it's cool, man, it's cool!" Stu spit on his finger and rubbed a little dab of bird poop off the hood.

It was true, Duff knew it: people would pay a lot to be cool. He himself, though he ordinarily looked down on people who worried about coolness, had enjoyed the admiring looks the car attracted.

But not enough to want to own the thing. As they drove away from the gas station, Duff allowed his eyes to flick to the rearview mirror every now and then. A blackish haze was still drifting from the end of the car. Behind him, other cars dropped back or passed him so they wouldn't be in its path. They rolled up their windows. Driving this car made Duff feel cool on the one hand and like a criminal on the other. Weren't there cars that ran on electricity? Or hydrogen, or something? He'd heard of cars like this, vaguely, but never seen one. Probably they weren't cool at all.

He sighed. He stretched out his left leg and straightened up in the seat. His muscles were getting stiff from sitting so long in the same position. They were approaching the outskirts of Louisville, Kentucky, now. More cars were on the road. It was nearly seven o'clock.

"How long till we get to St. Louis?" Stu asked.

"Maybe four hours."

"Well, let's have some dinner pretty soon, then. I'm starving."

They got off the highway and looked for a place to eat. There wasn't much. Finally they saw a hand-painted sign that read PETE'S STEWPOT, 5 MILES AHEAD—DOWN HOME COOKING.

"That sounds all right," Stu said.

But when they got there, the place didn't look inviting. It was a low, windowless brick building with a herd of motorcycles parked outside, their shiny black bodies glinting in the light from a neon beer sign on the wall. Duff hesitated.

"Let's go," said Stu, slinging his backpack over his shoulders and climbing out of the car.

Duff was hungry, so he followed.

Chapter 6
THE BIKERS' DANCE

Inside Pete's Stewpot it was so dark that they had to stand at the doorway for a minute to let their eyes adjust. The place seemed to be full of people, not sitting quietly in small groups at separate tables but roaming all around the room, calling out to one another, moving from one table to another. Someone was laughing a deep rumbling laugh. Loud music was playing. Duff realized that all these people were wearing either black leather jackets decorated with studs and chains or black T-shirts that said EAT MY DUST on the back. Most of them were men. A few were girls.

"Bikers," said Stu.

"Maybe we should try somewhere else," said Duff.

"There isn't anywhere else. I'm hungry. They won't bother us."

A large blond woman with a double chin emerged from the darkness and led them to a table back by the kitchen door. "Don't mind this crowd," she said. "They act tough but they're all right."

Duff wasn't sure about that. From painful personal experience, he knew that people like himself were tempting targets for people like these. The tougher they acted, the more pleasure they seemed to get out of persecuting defenseless computer geniuses. He put his menu up in front of his face and hunkered down low in his chair.

The bikers stared at them, sizing them up. A guy with a red bandanna tied around his forehead walked past their table and said, "How ya doin'?" in a way that didn't seem entirely friendly. The music stopped for a moment, and in the sudden quiet they heard someone give the punch line of a rowdy joke, and someone else said, "Hey, Sluggo, don't be crude, we got some nice boys in here tonight." Everyone in the room looked over at them. Duff concentrated on the menu.

The large blond woman reappeared and jotted down their order—spaghetti for Stu, a tuna sandwich for Duff. Duff read the name on her badge—KAY— and thought of his mother. If she could see him right now, having dinner in a biker hangout with a hitchhiker, she wouldn't be pleased.

"I'd like to have one of those big roadhog bikes some day," said Stu.

"Do they cost a lot?"

"Oh, yeah. I'd have to save up. But I ought to be able to get a good job in San Diego. That's where I'm headed. I can live with this buddy of mine for a while, so I won't have to pay rent."

"How come you're going all the way to California to get a job?" Duff said. "You could work on cars anywhere. You could get a job at home."

Stu held up his hands as if warding off a blow. "*Oh,*

no," he said. "*Oh*, no no no. Not at home with the mom and dad, no thank you. I aim to put a whole continent between me and them."

"Why?"

"*Because*, man. They want to chain me up! They wanted me to join the *military*, if you can believe that. Can you picture it? Me marching along in some kind of formation, wearing a uniform, with my hair all buzzed off?"

Duff shook his head. He couldn't picture it. "Why'd they want you to do that? Were you getting in trouble or something?"

Their food arrived, and Stu became very involved in sprinkling cheese on his spaghetti and wrapping strands of pasta around his fork. He seemed to have forgotten Duff's question, so Duff asked it again. He thought he deserved to know. "Were you getting in trouble?" he said.

Stu flapped his hand back and forth as if shooing away a fly. "Little stuff. Nothing major. People overreact." He took a big mouthful of spaghetti, shlooping up the dangling strands. "Hey, look what's going on," he said.

The music was blasting forth again, and a couple of the girls had started dancing. They weren't dancing *with* anyone, they just stepped out between the tables and waggled their hips and pumped their elbows back and forth. Whistles and catcalls came from the men. This went on for quite a while. It was too noisy to talk. Duff finished his sandwich; Stu scraped up the last of his spaghetti sauce with a piece of bread. "Let's go," said Stu.

Duff was standing at the counter, paying the bill, when he felt a tap on his shoulder. He turned around. A girl with purple eye shadow and ink-black hair was standing behind him. She smiled. "Hey, nice boy," she said. "Come on and dance with me."

"Oh, uh, no thanks," Duff said. "We were just leaving. . . ."

The girl put on a hurt expression. She grabbed his arm. "Come on," she said. "Just one little dance."

"No, really, we have to go." Duff pulled away. He had to get out of here.

"Anyway, he doesn't know how to dance," said Stu. "Otherwise, I'm sure he'd be delighted—"

A hand clamped onto Duff's shoulder. He spun around. The man with the bandanna was standing over him, scowling. "Boy," he said, "when my lady wants to dance with you, you dance."

What followed was about the worst five minutes in Duff's entire life so far. He was hauled out into the middle of the crowded room, where he wriggled wretchedly, humiliated down to his bones, while the girl flounced around him and the circle of bikers roared and jeered. When the music ended, the girl blew him a kiss, and Duff made a wild dash for the door and stumbled out into the parking lot. "Over here," called Stu, who was in the driver's seat of the car. Duff climbed in, breathing hard.

"Give me the keys, I'll drive," Stu said. Duff handed them over, and Stu hit the gas.

After a few miles, when he had more or less stopped shaking, Duff said, "Barbarians. Troglodytes. Neanderthals."

"Maybe," said Stu. "But you know, man, it's better if you lighten up around it. When you let them get to you, they get meaner. You gotta just laugh."

Duff scowled. Why should people who were dumb and mean have so much power over people who were smart and decent? What *was* it about him that made people like jocks and bikers want to pounce on him, as if they were wolves and he were a rabbit? Did he look like a rabbit? No. Did he act like a rabbit? No. He just wanted to be left alone to be his own slightly unusual self. What was so wrong with that?

Stu flicked on the radio, which was playing something with a lot of doo-wops in it. "That's enough oldies," Stu said. "Let's get up to date." He spun the radio dial with a practiced hand, passing over a talk show ("If you think I would *ever* let my child see a movie like that, then you—"), and a news report ("... on their way to clean up oil-soaked birds after a major spill off the coast of—"), and in a second he'd tuned in some fast, loud music with a pounding beat. He snapped his head back and forth in time to the rhythm and jerked his elbows around. "I love this one, man," he said. He joined in with it, shouting the words.

Duff stared straight ahead. He was not in the mood for music, especially music like this, which made him anxious. It reminded him of the one time he'd gone to a high school dance, which he only did because Kelly McMartin, who lived down the street from him and was in his calculus class, asked him to. When the music started up, and kids began to twitch and shuffle and bump against each other, a feeling of terror came over Duff. He didn't know how to do that twitching. He didn't want to do it. Fortunately, Kelly didn't seem set on doing it, either, so they sat near the drinks table most of the evening and, in the moments when the music stopped, he entertained her by explaining an interesting command structure he'd developed for his latest project.

"Don't you like this song?" said Stu, noticing Duff's silence.

"Not really," said Duff.

"Well, what *do* you like? I'll find some of your kind of music."

"My kind of music isn't on the radio," said Duff. "I brought my CDs. You can listen to those if you want to."

He turned around and groped in the back until he found his CD player and a CD called "Android Troop Loop." He put the CD in and handed the headphones to Stu.

Stu listened. After about a minute, the corner of his mouth pulled down and his eyes swiveled toward Duff. "What *is* this?" he said. "It sounds like a bunch of machines screaming at each other."

"Highly complex computer-generated effects," said Duff.

"Oh," said Stu. "I thought you said it was music."

"It is to me," said Duff.

Stu took the headphones off. They rode in silence for the next hour or so. Duff started to worry. He worried that he'd have trouble finding Rosalie Hopgood's house. He worried that they'd be arriving a lot later than they said they would. This morning, when he'd felt so smart and confident, seemed like eons ago. Now everything was going wrong. And Stu—he didn't know what to think about Stu. Sometimes he was glad he'd picked him up. Sometimes, like right now, he was sorry. If he hadn't been with Stu, he would have walked right out of Pete's Stewpot as soon as he walked in.

At last they were approaching St. Louis. Duff saw the lights of the city ahead of them. They came to a bridge over the wide Mississippi River. "We need some money for the toll," Stu said.

Duff reached into his pocket. He slid his fingers around but could not locate his wallet. He reached into his other pocket. No wallet there, either. This couldn't be true. He tried his back pockets. He jammed his hand down into the space between the seat and the seat back. He bent over and felt the floor by his feet.

"What's the problem?" said Stu.

"My wallet is gone." Duff's whole body slumped, as if his bones had turned to rubber. "I must have left it in that restaurant."

"Oh, no, man, that's awful. We'll stop and call them."

"No," said Duff, in a voice heavy with gloom. "It won't be there. It'll be in some biker's pocket by now. It'll be speeding down the road on a motorcycle."

"Not necessarily," Stu said. "You could have just left it on the counter or something. They can find it and send it to you."

"Send it where?" said Duff. "I don't know where I'm going to be."

"Hmm." Stu pondered, drumming his fingers on the steering wheel. "I guess we better turn around and go back for it."

"No," said Duff. "We're late delivering this car already. Anyway, it would be useless." Duff turned his face to the window. He felt as dark as the night sky. He knew he would never see his wallet again.

Chapter 7
THE CRIMINAL'S DEN

Stu paid the bridge toll, and they crossed the river and drove through the streets of the city. In the light from the streetlamps, Duff saw crumbling brick buildings and warehouses, but he wasn't interested in the scenery anymore. "How am I going to get money with no bank card?" he said. "And how am I going to keep going with no driver's license?"

"Keep going?" Stu said. "I thought St. Louis was your final destination."

"No," Duff said. "This is just where I drop off the

car. I have to get to California—San Jose."

"Oh, I get it," Stu said. "You didn't want to tell me *you* were heading for California, too, in case you didn't want to take me the whole way."

Duff didn't answer.

"No problem," said Stu. "I understand. You probably couldn't tell, just from meeting me once, what a delightful traveling companion I would be."

"Right," said Duff glumly. He couldn't help it if he was hurting Stu's feelings. It wasn't Stu's fault he'd been robbed, but his loathing of the bikers was so huge that it spread out like a black cloud, and some of it got on Stu.

"So why California?" Stu said.

"I have a job there. Silicon Valley. I'm going to be a programmer at a software company. They recruited me, sight unseen."

"A programmer," Stu said. "You mean where you go to an office and sit at a computer all day?"

"Correct," said Duff.

"Weird," Stu said. "You never know what people are going to like."

Duff reached up and turned on the overhead light. He read the directions written down by Carl, and Stu followed them, turning left and right through a maze of dark streets.

Finally, on a wide, busy avenue, they pulled up in front of a shabby brick house with a square of dead lawn in front. "This is it," Duff said. "Thirty-six seventy-five Waldo Avenue. We're later than I thought we'd be. I hope someone's still up."

It didn't look promising. The windows of the house were all dark. They went up the path, and Duff rang the doorbell. There was a burst of furious barking, and the door shook in its frame. After a few seconds, the porch light went on.

A voice called, "Who is it?"

"Duff Pringle, delivering the car," said Duff.

"Who?" The voice seemed disconcerted. "Wait a second."

They waited. In a minute, the door opened. Behind it was a girl wearing a big white T-shirt and skinny green pants. She was bent over sideways, holding on to the collar of a small, hairy, pointy-eared brown dog barking like a machine gun, *wow-wow-wow-wow*, and trying to lunge toward Duff's kneecaps. The girl had a round face, but there was a squareness to her jaw that made her look stubborn, or hard, or maybe angry. She appeared to be about sixteen. She stared at them, and then she stared past them at the car parked by the curb.

"Oh," she said. "My mom's car."

A seizure of shyness had come over Duff at the sight of this girl, but he managed to speak in a nearly normal voice. "Correct," he said.

"I thought Carl was bringing it," said the girl.

"He was too busy," said Duff.

"Doing what? He never does anything."

"There was going to be a party," Duff said. "He had a girl with him, named Angie."

"My mother better never hear about that," the girl said. "She'd kill him."

The dog made a desperate yelp and pulled against the girl's grasp. Its little toenails scrabbled on the floor.

"Shut up, Moony," said the girl. She picked it up with one arm and held it against her hip.

Stu said, "Your mother owes us—I mean him—fifty dollars."

"Well, she's not here," said the girl. "She's in the hospital. In Virginia. That's why she asked my grungy cousin to bring back the car."

"Oh," said Duff. "Sorry to hear that."

"I don't know where I'm supposed to get fifty dollars," she said.

For a minute or so, they all stood staring at one another. The girl looked frazzled, Duff thought. There were dirty paw smudges on her white T-shirt, and her blondish hair was in a style you might call get-out-of-my-face: some of it was yanked up on top of her head and bound with a fuzzy green rubber band, and the rest was stuck behind her ears.

She was frowning at them. They were probably the last straw for her in a day full of bad surprises.

Finally Duff said, "I guess we should take our stuff out of the car." He was seriously peeved about not getting his fifty dollars—especially since he now had zero dollars in his pocket.

"Okay," said the girl.

Nobody moved. Out on the street, someone honked a car horn, and brakes squealed.

The girl shifted the dog to her other hip. "So are you going?" she said.

"Yeah," said Stu.

"Where?" said the girl.

Duff and Stu looked at each other. "I don't know," they said, both at once.

"Well, you can't stay here," said the girl, "because I don't know you from a hole in the wall."

"Oh, well, no," Duff said, "I mean, of course you couldn't . . . we couldn't . . ."

Stu pushed past Duff and held out his hand. "I'm Stu Sturvich," he said. "Traveling companion of Duff Pringle, here. He's on his way to California to become a slave in Silicon Valley."

"A slave?" said the girl, giving Duff a curious look.

"That's right," said Stu, before Duff could protest.

"He's planning to crouch over a computer screen for the rest of his life, chained by the ankle to his desk, with his skin turning green from computer radiation and his fingers stiffening into claws and his legs dropping off from lack of use."

"Oh," said the girl. "That sounds fun."

"This is not true," said Duff. "Totally false. I have a good job at a software company." It didn't sound glamorous, he had to admit. "A really hot company," he added.

"Oh," said the girl. Then she said, "I'm Bonnie. And this is Moony. He's a good dog, but strangers get him upset."

Stu swept on. "I myself am going out west to ride the waves," he said. "I am looking for the perfect curl. California is our goal, but tonight we find ourselves temporarily without transportation. Or shelter."

"But if there's a campground or something nearby . . . ," said Duff. "Or a motel. . . Maybe you could take us there"—he gestured toward the car— "and drop us off?"

"Or," said Stu, "maybe we could just stretch out

under a bush in your nice backyard. We are harmless guys. Really. Tired, harmless guys who aren't getting their fifty dollars."

Bonnie regarded them, narrowing her eyes and crimping one corner of her mouth. Duff noticed, as he waited for her to say something, that she had a little gold star in one ear and a star and a moon in the other. She was a cute girl, he thought, though of course not his type, though actually he didn't really have a type, since the two girls he'd liked so far had been utterly different from each other, so how would he know if this girl was his type or wasn't?

"How about this," said Bonnie. "My mom converted the garage into sort of a workshop. You could stay there tonight. There's a couch, but one of you would have to sleep on the floor. But it's better than sleeping under a bush."

"Oh," said Duff, "that's really—that's—I guess—"

"Great!" said Stu. He grabbed Duff's arm and yanked him backward down the steps. "We'll get our stuff from the car."

• • •

Rosalie Hopgood's workshop still looked quite a bit like a garage. The floor was concrete, pipes and wires snaked along the walls, and some cobwebby cardboard cartons were stacked in a corner. The workshop part occupied another corner, where a turquoise rug had been laid over the concrete. At one edge of the rug was a couch covered in faded salmon-colored velvet, and at another edge was a desk made of a door and two file cabinets. On the desk was a computer, a fairly new one. Rosalie Hopgood must be in business of some kind.

Bonnie, who had left Moony in the house, sat down on the couch and folded her legs underneath her. "This is where my mom does her projects," she said.

"What sort of projects?" asked Stu.

"Oh . . . kind of . . . creative projects," said Bonnie.

"Writing?"

"Uh-huh."

"Wow, that's great," said Stu. "Is she famous?"

Bonnie laughed. There was a note of bitterness in

her laugh, Duff thought. "Right now," Bonnie said, "she's a little more famous than she wants to be."

Stu looked at her with his eyebrows raised. His whole expression radiated interest, just the way it had when Duff first met him and he asked about Duff's work. This guy is good at making people like him, Duff thought.

"Tell me more," Stu said.

Bonnie smiled her half smile. She grabbed hold of her toes—she was barefoot, and her toenails were painted gold—and held on to them for a few seconds, staring down at her lap. "I told her she'd get in trouble," she said. "She thought she was being so clever." She looked up. "I don't see why I shouldn't tell you. What difference could it make?"

She crossed to the computer and flicked it on: a few clicks of the mouse, and she had an e-mail message on the screen. "Read this," she said. "It's one of her best ones."

Duff and Stu bent over to peer at the screen.

They read:

Dear friends,

I am crying so hard I can barely type this, but you are my only hope. Last week, while my back was turned for one instant, my darling two-year-old son Timmy toddled out into the highway that runs past our crumbling cottage and was sucked under the wheels of a gigantic oil tanker truck. I ran to him, screaming. His limp, mangled body lay in a bloody heap on the pavement.

Oh, my friends, the tiny crushed bones!!! The blood pouring from hundreds of gashes all over the sweet little body!!! Timmy survived, but it's going to take 27 separate operations to make him look like a little boy again instead of a squashed eggplant.

I am a penniless single mom, working 15 hours a day as a raisin picker, and I can't possibly pay for his treatment. Will you help me? Oh, please! I would be so grateful for anything you could send—even just a dollar or two. My address is P.O. Box 22569B, St. Louis, MO 63321.

In desperation,

Melissa Lu Perkins

Duff turned to Bonnie, his mouth hanging open in amazement. "You mean people actually sent her money?"

"Yeah, lots of people. I think just on this one she made a couple thousand dollars. She has a whole collection of them. The one about her husband getting both arms gnawed off by a wild boar is a good one, too."

"People are stupid," said Duff.

Bonnie shrugged. "Or kind. They were trying to help."

"She shouldn't have said 'raisin picker,'" Duff added. "You don't pick raisins, you pick grapes."

"That's true," Bonnie said. She laughed and flashed a smile at him—a real smile, not just a polite one. It made the clamped-down, worried look vanish from her face for a moment, and it caused a little burst of tingles inside Duff, who wasn't used to making girls smile.

"That's a rotten thing to do, taking advantage of people who feel sorry for you," said Stu, jabbing a finger at the computer screen.

"I know," said Bonnie. "It isn't the first time, either. A few years ago she was into real estate. A lot of people made down payments on islands in the South Pacific that weren't exactly there. She was in for two years that time."

"In?" said Duff.

"In jail," said Bonnie. "For fraud."

"But I thought you said she was in the hospital."

"She is." Bonnie flopped down on the couch. She gave a wry half smile. "She broke her left leg and her right arm."

"How'd she do *that*?" Stu asked.

"Going too fast down the back stairs of this office she rents in Virginia," said Bonnie. "When she saw the fraud squad coming up the front stairs."

Duff listened to all this in amazement. He was in a criminal's den! Bonnie was a criminal's daughter! She didn't look it. He would have expected a criminal's daughter to be the sort of girl who hides razor blades in her hair, and gets into fistfights in the girls' restroom, and talks in a nasty, sneering voice. Bonnie didn't seem to be that kind of person. She did have that hint of hardness in her face, like a warning that she would take no crap from anyone, but mostly she just seemed sort of weary and fed up. He wished he could think of something helpful to say.

"How come your mom was in Virginia?" Stu asked.

"Oh, she works out of all different places. It makes her harder to trace."

Stu sat down cross-legged on the turquoise rug near Bonnie's feet. "So what about you?" he said. "With your mom away, what will you do? Live here by yourself?"

"Are you kidding? The social worker would be on me in a second. No, I'll go stay with one of my aunts." She reached up with both hands and yanked at her little topknot, which had been coming loose from its fuzzy rubber band. "I have two aunts," she said, "one in New Mexico and one in Los Angeles. My mother's sisters. I haven't seen either one of them since I was about eight, but I know they'd have me."

"So you'll drive your mom's car?" Stu asked.

"No. I don't have a driver's license. I'll probably go on the bus." She unfolded her legs and stood up. "How are you going to get where *you're* going?"

"I don't know," said Stu. "Go back to hitchhiking, maybe."

Duff shook his head. "Not me," he said. "Too slow. I have to figure out some other way." He suddenly remembered that he had no money and no driver's license, not to mention no car, and for a moment he felt so depressed he couldn't even breathe.

Phone Call #2

Thursday, June 27, 1:12 AM

Duff: Hi, Dad, it's me.

Duff's father: Duff. Good lord. Do you know it's two in the morning here?

Duff: Oh, yeah, sorry. I didn't think. I'm in St. Louis, just wanted to let you know.

Duff's father: St. Louis! That's over eight hundred miles from here!

Duff: Yeah, well, I wanted to get as far as I could my first day.

Duff's father: And where are you?

Duff: Oh, a motel. It's, uh, the Hopgood.

Duff's father: And you had no trouble on the way? Car worked okay?

Duff (telling the biggest lie of his life): Oh, yeah, no problems.

Duff's father: Well, good, Son. Maybe you're going to prove me wrong after all. I was sure you'd get

into some kind of mess your first day out and
come running back.

Duff (piling lie on lie): Oh, no, Dad, I'm doing fine.

Duff's father: I called Wade Belcher and told him
you'd be getting in touch.

Duff (thinks): *Not likely.* **(says):** Okay, Dad. Talk to
you later.

Chapter 8
READY TO ROLL

It was already hot when Duff woke in the morning.
The garage door was open, and Stu wasn't around.
Duff stepped outside. Cars went past in a steady
stream. The air was hazy and smelled like cleaning
fluid. Duff thought again about what Phil at the gas
station had said about noxious chemicals. He could
feel them at this very moment, seeping into his lungs.
What the world needs, he thought grouchily, is a car
that runs on air.

He went back inside and opened up his laptop. No

problem with his wireless connection here in the city. Maybe, by some miracle, his e-mail would give him an answer to his predicament. Instead he found this:

Dear Duffy:

Gearing up here! Project Rapid Vortex is ready to roll. Just to let you know—had to cut a couple other projects. Budgets are tight!! But Vortex is top priority!!! Looking forward to getting you on board—see you Monday!!!!

Ping

Ping's e-mail voice was exactly the same as his real voice—speedy, energetic, and excited. He was a fast-paced person, Duff thought, probably the kind of person who wouldn't be too pleased if his newly hired programmer didn't make it to work on the first day. Right now, Thursday, June 27, Duff had no car, no cash, and no driver's license. He was still probably two thousand miles away from San Jose. Several miracles would have to occur for him to get to California by

Monday. But sometimes miracles did happen. So he wrote this note:

Dear Ping,
I'll be there.
Duff

This looked unfriendly compared to Ping's e-mail, so he added a few exclamation points:

Dear Ping,
I'll be there!!
Duff

He clicked Send, closed his laptop, and went outside again, feeling like one of those cartoon characters with a black cloud hovering over his head. Hearing voices, he looked into the backyard, where he saw Moony nosing around in the grass and Stu and Bonnie sitting on the back steps of the house, eating something. Also laughing. A stab of unpleasant feeling went through

Duff. Why hadn't they asked him to come and eat something, too?

Moony charged at him and barked at his ankles as he approached.

"Hey," said Bonnie. "Want a bagel?"

"Thanks." There didn't seem to be any more room on the steps, so Duff stood looking down at them. Today Bonnie had her hair in two sproutlike ponytails, one over each ear. She was wearing shorts. She had very smooth knees and her legs were tanned. She handed him an onion bagel.

"Sleep all right?" she said.

"Moderately well." Duff sat down on the grass.

"We've been talking about music," said Stu. "It's a big part of Bonnie's life."

"Interesting," said Duff, wondering how Stu had learned big things about Bonnie in such a small time.

"I write songs," said Bonnie. "And sing."

"And she plays the guitar," said Stu. "She's heading for the big time." He clapped a hand on Bonnie's shoulder, and Duff felt a sudden hatred for him.

"Listen," Duff said. "We have to figure out what to do. I have to get moving."

"Don't get in a tizz," Stu said. "It's all figured out."

"It is?"

Bonnie answered him. "I called Shirley this morning—my aunt in Albuquerque—and told her I'm coming. Stu said what if you guys drove my mom's car and we all went together?" She smiled at Duff and then flipped the last bite of her bagel out onto the grass, where Moony instantly snapped it up.

Duff felt the black cloud dissolve. Stu was useful after all! Of course, there was still the problem of his missing money and driver's license, but he'd solve that somehow. Make Stu do all the driving. Maybe he'd have time to stop in at a bank and see if he could get his card replaced. "Great!" he said. "When do we leave?"

"This evening," said Stu. "It's going to be a scorcher today, and that Chevy has no air-conditioning. Better to drive at night."

Just then Duff heard footsteps crunching up the

driveway, and a voice said crossly, "Oh, there you are. I rang the doorbell, but I guess you didn't hear me."

Duff whipped around. A short, stout old woman was coming toward them at a determined pace. She wore a baggy lavender-flowered dress, a flat straw sun-hat, and flip-flops that slapped against her heels with every step.

"Hi, Wanda," said Bonnie.

Wanda glared at Duff and Stu. Then she glared at Bonnie and said, "How's your poor mother?"

"Doing okay," said Bonnie.

"Broke her leg, you said?"

"And her arm."

Wanda shook her head and looked grim. "You'd better come over and stay with me while your mother's away," she said. "Can't live here by yourself." She cast another dark look at Duff and Stu, but Bonnie didn't introduce them.

"I'm going to my aunt Shirley's," said Bonnie. "Mom knows. I called her yesterday. Thanks anyhow."

"Well," said Wanda. She stood there, not moving.

Duff could tell she was waiting for more information. The sun shone through the straw of her hat and mottled her face. She looked, Duff thought, the way a toadstool would look if it were a human being. "Who're your friends?" she said at last.

"Duff and Stu," said Bonnie.

Wanda made a kind of grumphing sound. She stood there a little longer, but Bonnie just gazed at her serenely, and finally she turned to go. "Give my regards to your mother," she said, and stumped off down the driveway.

"The neighbor," said Bonnie when she was gone. "The idea of staying with her . . ." She shuddered. Clearly the idea was too awful to put into words.

Duff decided that since he had a whole day here in St. Louis, he might as well see some of those famous sights he'd read about, and maybe get some exercise at the same time. He asked Bonnie for directions, put on his running shoes, and headed for the Mississippi to see the Gateway Arch.

He was so hot when he got there that he flopped down on the grass beneath the arch and viewed it from a horizontal position. It was huge, bigger than it looked in pictures. It soared up higher than the multi-story buildings nearby. The Mississippi River flowed along beside it, carrying barges and tourist boats, and for a moment Duff thought about the travelers who had come through there two hundred years ago, also on their way to the West Coast, journeying not in cars but on foot and horseback. (He thought for a second about horse emissions, so different from car emissions.) It would have been a rough trip, he thought. Engine breakdowns and thieving bikers were nothing compared with what those pioneer guys went through.

For a while, he wandered along the riverbank, watching the tourists and the boats, forgetting momentarily about his troubles. He thought how nice it must have been back in riverboat days to float along with only the sound of the water rippling, or the paddle wheel turning, or whatever sound a riverboat made. Did riverboats have fumes, he wondered? What did they run on? Steam? But what heated the water to make the steam? Coal? His mind roamed pleasantly.

He got back to Bonnie's house around four o'clock. Sounds were coming from inside. Voices, and laughing. He went up the steps and rapped on the door. "Hullo?" he called. No one answered. Then a blast of noise came at him so hard he nearly fell backward. It was music, he realized after a second. He opened the door and groped forward through the firestorm of sound. He made it to the living room, where he saw Stu and Bonnie flinging their arms around and moving in little jerks. Dancing together! Looking like morons.

He knocked on the door frame to get their attention. "Hey!" he yelled. They looked at him in surprise and stopped dancing. They turned off the music.

"Hi," said Bonnie. "Do you like Hairy Oatmeal?"

Duff was hungry, but not that hungry. "No, thank you," he said. "Why don't we just order a pizza?"

Stu and Bonnie broke into shrieks of laughter. "No, no, it's the group, it's their name, Hairy Oatmeal," Bonnie cried. "They're so great, don't you think?"

Duff felt a horrible blush heating up his face. "No," he said. "I think they sound like dying roosters."

"Who do you like, then?" Bonnie was breathing fast from dancing. Her face was rosy, and one of her ponytails had slipped out of its rubber band.

Duff was so mad and embarrassed that he said the first thing that came into his head. "Right now I like Hot Triple-Cheese Pizza, and I like Ice Cold Jumbo Coke, and I think Basket of Fries with Ketchup is pretty good, too."

"Hey, he *does* have a sense of humor," said Stu. "Let's order some dinner."

The pizza came an hour later. Salad, too—Bonnie said people couldn't live just on pizza and bagels, they had to have green things at least now and then. Stu paid for the food, and they ate it sitting on the living-room floor. It was an odd living room, Duff thought. It looked as if Bonnie's mother had started to furnish it and then lost interest. In one corner was a huge shiny television and sound system, and in the opposite corner was a brown armchair of the kind that leans back and puts out a footrest when you pull a lever. There was a coffee table made of a chunk of wood and a sheet of glass. But other than those things, the room was more or less empty. Some limp cushions lay on the floor, two folding chairs, folded up, leaned against the wall, and a striped bedsheet hung over the window for a curtain. The room looked as if whoever lived here had not quite finished moving in, or else was about to move out.

Stu told a long, involved story. It had to do with some friend of his who used to know the brother of the drummer in Hairy Oatmeal, and how this brother was a skateboard pro who traveled all over doing exhibitions, and how Stu himself had been to Baltimore and met either the brother or the drummer, Duff couldn't tell which because he wasn't really listening. He was watching Bonnie pluck at the long strings of cheese that looped from her pizza to her mouth, and he was trying to think of something *he* could talk about if Stu would ever shut up.

"So," Stu said, "I really got to know those guys.

They said I could come and stay in their penthouse anytime." He took a bite of his pizza. Some tomato sauce dribbled down his chin, and he had to stop talking for a moment to wipe it off.

Duff seized the opportunity. "Yeah," he said. "I've been to Baltimore, too. I went there for this conference about games and entertainment and, you know, lifestyle stuff. Mostly I went to the part about games, because that's my—that's what I'm going to be doing. In my new job. But also they had this expo about twenty-first century electronics. Where they showed how things are going to be in the future." He took a gulp of air and kept going. "Your house will have chips built in, so when you come home it'll say hello to you, and turn on the lights for you, and make the air smell like whatever you want—like, you know, pine trees, or ocean or whatever you like. And robots will fix your dinner and clean the floors and play chess with you. Or you could, like, have a sword fight with a hologram opponent. And your wallpaper will turn different colors to match what mood you're in. And you'll even have chips implanted under your skin, so you'll be able to download your thoughts right from your brain onto your computer." He glanced at Bonnie to see if she was amazed. He couldn't tell.

"Nobody better put a computer chip under *my* skin," said Stu. "They could track you, with one of those. They'd always be able to find you."

"Who would?" Bonnie said.

"The authorities," Stu said darkly.

Bonnie sighed. She picked some crumbs off the floor and folded up the pizza box. "Well," she said to Duff as she walked toward the kitchen, "hope you have fun doing all that."

It was after seven o'clock. They'd decided to leave at eight-thirty, so Duff had a little time to kill. He checked his e-mail again—nothing of interest—and then, just for fun, typed "car that runs on air" into his search engine. He found this:

A French engineer named Guy Negre has invented a car called the e.Volution that runs on air. Compressed air pumped into the vehicle's tanks is slowly released to power pistons that drive the car. A fill-up at an "air station" takes three minutes, and a fully pumped e.Volution can travel about 120 miles for a mere 30 cents. The car's only tailpipe emission is air.

Incredibly cool, Duff thought. The more he read about it, the more interested he got. His mind ticked off the possibilities, and pretty soon he was fixing the entire world. No more oil lights on dashboards. No more thrown rods, or noxious fumes, or wars over oil-rich countries. No more oil-drenched birds. All the cars on the freeways puffing out clean air, changing the earth's atmosphere. It really grabbed his imagination—so much so that he found the engineer's e-mail address and fired off a note to him:

Dear Sir,
The air car is totally brilliant. I wish I had one right now, as I am driving to California for my new programming job in a car that has serious emissions problems. If

everyone had an air car instead of a gas car, what a
different world.

Yours truly,

Duff Pringle

He closed up his laptop. He was full of energy—
excited by his interesting discovery, eager to get on the
road again, and (he had to admit it) stirred up by little
tinglings of attraction toward Bonnie. All this surged
around inside him and made him feel as if the programs in his body were running too fast—the heart
program, the lungs program, the brain program—and
if he sat still with all that going on in him, his whole
system would crash. If he'd been at home, he would
have gotten on his bike and taken a long, fast ride.
Instead he decided to take a quick run around the
block, since he was going to have to sit still for the next
several hours.

He went out to the sidewalk and started running.
He ran about the same speed as the traffic on the street,
which was backed up because of a fender bender up

ahead, and when he came to a corner he turned right, and at the next corner right again. He went around the whole block twice.

He was breathing hard when he got back to the house. For a moment, he stood still by the steps. The front door was open, and so were the front windows, but he didn't hear any sounds of movement inside the house. So he went up the driveway toward the back-yard, where he saw Bonnie sitting on the grass by a big lilac bush. He could tell she hadn't heard him coming. Her arms were wrapped around Moony, who was curled up on her lap, and her face was pressed against the thick brown fur on Moony's back. Duff stopped. Something told him Bonnie might not want to talk right now. He was about to head quietly to the garage—but Moony, who must have heard his feet crunching on the gravel, burst into his machine-gun bark, and Bonnie jolted upright and looked straight at Duff.

Her face was streaked with tears.

Duff was instantly paralyzed. Crying! What did you

say to someone who was crying? He had no idea. Should he just go away? Or would that seem unkind? Or was it unkind to stand there staring? He didn't know. His legs had turned into concrete.

Bonnie dumped Moony off her lap. She stood up and slapped the grass blades off the seat of her shorts. Then she glared at Duff. There were red splotches under her eyes. "What are *you* lookin' at?" she said, and she stomped across the lawn, climbed the back steps, and went inside, slamming the door behind her.

Chapter 9

AN ALL-NIGHT DRIVE

Duff was confused. Bonnie had been fine when he went out for his run. What could have upset her? Whatever it was, he'd probably made it worse by standing there gaping at her.

In the garage, Stu was cramming his belongings into his backpack. When he saw Duff, he straightened up and grinned at him.

"Hey, good news, man," he said. "I found your wallet."

"You *did*?"

"Yeah. Weirdest thing! It was in my backpack."

"What? How did it get there?"

Stu shrugged. "I don't know, but here's my guess. One of those bikers snatched it off the counter while you were dancing. Grabbed what he wanted out of it and stuck it in my pack. I didn't notice, because I was busy watching you."

A vision of himself dancing threatened to rise in Duff's imagination, and he shut it out. "What got taken?" he said.

"Just money. Everything else is there, looks like."

Duff took his wallet from Stu and sat down on the salmon-colored couch to examine it. What Stu said was true: his license was there, and his bank card, and his triple A card, and a few other things. All the money was gone except for forty-six cents. The biker who nabbed his wallet had gotten over three hundred dollars, which would probably be spent on chrome polish and beer. But Duff was so relieved to have his license and bank card back that he almost didn't care.

"I'm ready," said Stu, slinging his pack over one shoulder. "Are you?"

Duff put his wallet in his pocket. He snapped closed his laptop and zipped his duffel. "Let's go."

They went out to the car, which was parked at the end of the driveway. Stu got in the driver's seat and honked the horn. The door of the house opened, and Bonnie stepped out.

She had a battered brown suitcase in one hand and her guitar case in the other. The setting sun shone in her face; she squinted her eyes against it. Duff wondered how she felt. Was she sad to be leaving her house? Or maybe angry at her mother for screwing up? He couldn't tell.

He opened the door on the passenger side of the car and then went over to Bonnie and took the suitcase, which he put in the trunk. Bonnie went back to the house and came out with a big plastic carrying case with a wire screen on one end. She set it down long enough to turn and lock the front door, and then she brought it to the car. "Moony has to ride in his crate," she said. "Otherwise, he jumps all over the place. Sometimes he gets carsick, too, so it's good if he isn't in anyone's lap when he does."

They got settled in the car. Bonnie sat in front. Duff sat in back next to Moony, who was turning round and round and pawing at an old ripped cushion Bonnie had provided for him. When he had his bedding properly arranged, he lay down, pressed his black nose against the wire mesh, and whimpered.

"Okay," said Stu. "Three, two, one, zero—blast off!" He floored the accelerator, and with a squeal of tires they were away.

Duff grabbed Moony's case to keep it steady. "Where are we heading?" he asked.

"Albuquerque, of course," Stu said. "Home of Bonnie's esteemed aunt Shirley."

"Yeah, but it'll take a couple days to get to Albuquerque," Duff said. "Where are we heading tonight?"

"First stop, Oklahoma City," Stu said. "We should be there by morning."

They drove. Stu and Duff took turns at the wheel. Whoever was in the passenger seat was supposed to make sure the driver didn't fall asleep, and whoever was in the backseat slept. Bonnie got less sleep than the other two, but she didn't seem to mind. When it was his turn to drive, Duff concentrated on the road, trying to keep his mind strictly blank, avoiding troubling questions such as: How long would it take to get from Albuquerque to San Jose? How was he going to get there without a car? How much did a plane ticket cost? He pushed all these thoughts aside and concentrated on the road.

When it was his turn to sleep, he lay uncomfortably on the backseat with his legs draped over Moony's crate, drifting in and out of an uneasy doze. It was a strange, dreamlike trip—the headlights approaching and passing like the eyes of big night animals, the hum of the motor, the long, rhythmic rumble of the wheels on the road. It was peaceful, in a way—no hard decisions to be made. Duff was almost sorry when light started to show around the edges of the sky.

They came into Oklahoma City hungry for breakfast. Once off the freeway, they wandered up and down city streets until Duff spotted a bank with an ATM machine, where he replenished his supply of cash. Not far from the bank was a fast-food place. They pulled in and parked. Bonnie took Moony for a short walk around the parking lot and served him his breakfast in the car. Then the three of them went inside. They ordered their food and flopped down at a table by the window.

Duff was tired but wired at the same time. It was interesting to be in a place he'd never seen before, even if it was, at least this part of it, a kind of uninteresting place. It looked pretty much like the outskirts of any other city, but because it was early morning and the sun was rising in a pinkish yellow haze and the air had a tingly smell that seemed a combination of gas fumes and freshly cut grass, everything had a feeling of shimmery newness.

They were all hungry. They concentrated on their eggs and hash browns and didn't talk much. Duff gazed out the window at the four lanes of morning traffic surging toward the stop light, halting, waiting while cars streamed across, starting again, stopping again, and on and on. All those people going off to work, he thought. Probably most of them heading for those tall buildings he could see from here. He imagined a little office cubicle behind each tiny glittering window, and—by nine o'clock or so—a little person in each cubicle, answering phone messages, reading e-mails, settling in for a day of work. That would be him, pretty soon.

Stu commented now and then on a passing car: "Nice Jag." "Classic Mustang—I could go for one like that." "Hey, look, a weird old Studebaker!"

So Duff stared at the cars, too, though he couldn't tell one kind from another, until something he saw written on the front end of a bus caught his attention. THIS BUS GETS 250 MILES PER ACRE, it said.

"What's that mean?" he asked Stu, pointing at the bus.

Stu squinted at it. "Miles per acre?" he said. "Mystery to me."

The bus turned the corner and drove past the restaurant. On its side, it said, SOYBEAN POWERED! THIS BUS RUNS ON SOYBEAN BIODIESEL. A picture of huge tan-colored round things that must be soybeans decorated the bus's whole lower half.

"Biodiesel," Duff said. "Do you know what that is?"

"Not really," said Stu, forking in his last bite of fried potatoes. "Diesel I know, but not biodiesel."

The bus stopped, sucked up the people waiting at the bus stop, and moved on. It seemed to be an ordinary city bus. How could it be running on soybeans? But if a car could run on air . . .

By the time Duff and the others had finished breakfast, a few more people were waiting at the bus stop outside. Duff couldn't resist asking one of them about the bean bus.

"Oh, yeah," said the guy he asked, a young man wearing a white shirt and tie and carrying his suit jacket under his arm. "We've got a fleet of them. They run on biodiesel. That's fuel made out of vegetable oil, you know?"

"It's not gas?" asked Duff.

"No, no. Like from beans or corn. The kind of oil you use to make french fries. You can make it out of *used* french fry oil, even."

Stu yelled from the parking lot. "Duffer! Hurry up!"

"Wait just a sec!" Duff called back. "Really?" he said to the guy. "Used *french fry oil*?"

Another bus pulled up to the stop and the passengers started to get on. The guy in the suit nodded and moved forward. Duff moved with him.

"But why?" he said.

The guy shrugged. "For diesel engines, it works just as well," he said. "And it doesn't pollute." He stepped up onto the bus and looked back at Duff. "Lots of cities have them," he said, "but we were one of the first."

The door slapped closed, and the bus pulled away, leaving Duff's mind humming again, as it had when he'd come across the air car. He thought about the thousands of fast-food places dotted across the nation. Maybe every single McDonald's and Burger King and Wendy's could turn their used oil into biodiesel, and they could all have little fuel stations out back, and then people with diesel cars, when they'd finished eating their hamburgers, could—

"DUFF!" It was Bonnie's voice this time. She and Stu were standing at the open doors of the car in the restaurant parking lot. "Get over here!"

Duff went. It was his turn to drive. But full stomachs made all of them sleepy. They'd spent the night more awake than not, and they needed to rest. So Duff drove until he found a good spot to park on a shady, out-of-the-way street. Bonnie took Moony for a short walk and then stretched out on the backseat of the car. Stu reclined the passenger seat as far as it would go and dozed off with his mouth open. Duff bunched up his jacket and leaned his head against the window, but he didn't have room to stretch his legs out, and his mind was still churning with the notion of cars running on french fry oil, so he didn't sleep much. By noon they were on the highway again, bound for Amarillo, Texas, where somehow they'd have to figure out a way to spend the night.

Phone Call #3

Friday, June 28, 11:35 AM

Wanda: Hello?

Rosalie Hopgood: Wanda, it's Rosalie. I've been trying to call Bonnie. No answer.
Do you know where she is?

Wanda: I do indeed. She drove off in your car last night with two boys.

Rosalie: Two boys? What boys?

Wanda: Sloppy-looking boys. One of them had long hair.

Rosalie: But *what* boys? Where did they come from?

Wanda: Don't shout, Rosalie. I don't know where they came from. They appeared, in your car, yesterday.

Rosalie: *They* appeared in my car! And now they've gone?

Wanda: Yes, gone to her aunt, Bonnie said.
Aunt Shirley.

Rosalie: She told me that. But she said she was

going to take the bus, leaving tomorrow.

What's she up to now?

Wanda: Listen, Rosalie, I really think that girl should—

Rosalie: Thank you, Wanda. Good-bye.

Phone Call #4

Friday, June 28, 11:38 AM

Burl (a close colleague of Rosalie Hopgood's): Hello?

Rosalie: Burl, I have a problem. Bonnie's taken off in the Chevy with two boys.

Burl: Oh, hi, Rosalie. Heard you got—

Rosalie: Did you hear what I said? That Chevy is out on the highway somewhere instead of safe in the driveway of my house.

Burl: Uh-huh.

Rosalie: And in the Chevy is a very significant bundle of cash.

Burl: Oh, from your last—

Rosalie: That's right. I want you and Rolf to go after it.

Burl: After the Chevy?

Rosalie: And Bonnie. She's with two boys! I want to know why.

Burl: But how do we find her?

Rosalie: She's heading for Shirley's, in Albuquerque. Four seventy-eight Cactus Wren Way. They left yesterday. Get going.

Burl: Now? But I was just—

Rosalie: Now. Ten percent of what's in the trunk if you bring the Chevy back safe. And Bonnie, too, of course.

Burl: Okay, okay, we're gone.

Chapter 10
A STU PROBLEM

All the way to Amarillo, Stu and Bonnie had a great time. Stu, who sat in the front seat, flicked on the radio as soon as they were out on the road. He found some music and turned it up loud, and he and Bonnie shouted along with it and bounced around in their seats. Duff didn't bounce. He didn't shout. He wished he were the sort of person who liked to bounce and shout, but he knew he couldn't pretend to be; it would look all wrong. Instead, between songs, he told them about how fast-food places could turn into gas stations, and he described a couple more of the computer games he'd created, the ones called Zoomball and Angry Alien Anteaters. Stu and Bonnie listened politely, and Bonnie said, "Amazing!" about the french fry fuel. Then they went back to their music.

After a while, Stu turned down the radio, crooked his elbow over the back of the seat, and twisted around to talk to Bonnie.

"Listen," he said, "I have a buddy in LA who's in the music business. Maybe he could help you some way."

"You think so? That would be great."

"Sure, he's in with lots of the groups. And the big companies, too, I think. We could meet up there, maybe, later on, and I could introduce you."

"Fantastic," said Bonnie.

"Also," Stu went on, "this friend of mine has connections to recording studios. You could make a demo, you know? And I could give it to him, and he could play it for the right people."

"Really?"

"Yeah."

"Cool. It's so good I met you, Stu."

"Hey, what about me?" said Duff. He meant to say it in a jolly, teasing way, but it came out as a wounded croak.

"Sure. You, too," Bonnie said. "Of course."

"This buddy of mine," said Stu, "the last time I talked to him, he was telling me about a guy who sent in a demo—no one had ever heard of him—and they liked it so much they offered him a contract before they even met him."

"You're kidding me," Bonnie said.

"No, really."

"That is so cool."

They went on like this. Duff was left out, which seemed unfair, since without him Stu would still be standing by the road with his thumb out. He wasn't *obliged* to take Stu anywhere. He could have left Stu in St. Louis to fend for himself. Probably should have, he thought sourly. Then he and Bonnie would be making this trip on their own. Would that be a bad thing or a good thing? Bad: talking to girls made him nervous. Good: he found Bonnie sort of interesting, even though (or because?) she was a criminal's daughter. He felt sorry for her, too. The image of her crying into Moony's neck fur stayed in his mind.

By four o'clock, they were rolling into Amarillo. Duff, who had driven the whole way, was seriously tired. Stu, who'd been having a great time, was full of energy. "Okay," he said. "How about we have a picnic? We get some sandwiches, we find a park, we eat. Then, with rested minds and satisfied stomachs, we figure out what to do next."

No one had a better plan, so that's what they did. They found a deli and bought food, and they found a park with a nice big lawn, crowded with picnickers and Frisbee players. It was all very festive, but Duff was too tired to enjoy it. After they'd eaten, he stretched out on the grass with his head on his duffel bag and closed his eyes. Let Stu and Bonnie figure out the next step of the journey. For the moment, he was checking out.

"Hey, wake up."

Duff's eyes sprang open, and he saw Bonnie standing

over him, nudging him with her toe. He sat up. "What's the matter?"

"Stu's gone," said Bonnie.

"Gone?" Duff felt a sudden lightness. He tried to keep himself from smiling.

"Yeah," Bonnie said. "It was weird. We were just sitting here, and all of a sudden he jumped up with this kind of scared look on his face and said, 'I gotta go.' So I said, 'Go where?' and he said he had to go get some cigarettes, he was all out. But I've never seen him smoke even once, have you?"

"Nope, not once."

"He said he'd be right back, and that was"—she looked at her watch—"that was over an hour ago."

"Maybe he just took off."

"But why would he do that? He *likes* me—us, I mean. He wants to travel with us."

Duff thought about this. Here was his chance to part ways with Stu. It would be easy. And no big tragedy for Stu—he had hitchhiked before he met Duff, he could hitchhike again. It would be justifiable, too. Why should they wait around for him if he was going to just disappear like this?

"Maybe something's happened to him," Bonnie said.

"Like what?"

"I don't know. Like he got hit by a car. Or he got lost. Or he got accidentally locked in the men's room or something."

Duff longed to leap to his feet, jump in the car with Bonnie, and be gone, leaving Stu to find his way alone. But he could think of three reasons not to. Reason one was Bonnie. Obviously, for some mysterious reason, she liked Stu and didn't want to abandon him. Reason two was that it was because of Bonnie that Duff wasn't still in St. Louis without a car. She had done him a favor, and he should do her one in return. Reason three was plain old human kindness. There was at least a remote possibility that Stu was in trouble and needed help. Yes, he was an annoying human being, and probably a dishonest one, but still he *was* one. And Duff had to admit that in spite of everything, he did like Stu a tiny bit. He was a cheerful guy, whatever else he might be.

"I guess we better wait till we find him," he said. "I guess we can't just leave him."

So they waited, sitting there in the park in the shade of a large tree. It would have been a good time to talk, if only Duff's shyness hadn't grabbed hold of him again. But now that Stu wasn't there chattering away, he couldn't think of what to talk about. He'd never mentioned having seen Bonnie crying in the backyard. She hadn't mentioned it, either. Was she sad about her mother? He thought about how he'd feel if his own mother were put in jail—arrested, say, for pouring hot coffee over some obnoxious patron at the restaurant, though that would be an extremely unlikely thing for his mild-mannered mother to do. But if it *had* happened, he'd feel all kinds of ways: mad at his mother for doing such a dumb thing, mad at the obnoxious customer, sad that his mother had to sit in some crummy jail, sorry for himself for being suddenly motherless. . . . Maybe Bonnie felt all that, too. How could he ask her about it?

She was sitting cross-legged, bending over and

pulling up grass blades. She pulled them slowly so they came out whole, and then she chewed a little on the whitish root part. She was close enough to Duff that he could smell something sort of sweet and toasty— maybe the suntan lotion she put on her legs. His mind raced, searching for words.

Finally he said, "Your mom, and everything . . . that must be . . . I mean, you must feel—"

But as soon as he spoke, Bonnie frowned at the ground and scrambled to her feet. "Don't talk to me about it," she said. "You don't know anything."

She stooped down to open the door of Moony's carrying case. He bounded out as if shot from a cannon, ran a few hundred feet in a straight line, and then ran back and leaped around Bonnie's feet. From inside the case, she fetched an ancient Day-Glo green tennis ball and threw it with a powerful overhand pitch. Moony raced after it.

Duff felt as if he'd had cold water splashed in his face. As usual, he'd said the wrong thing. Why hadn't he kept his mouth shut? He couldn't do human relations, he might as well just accept it. For a moment, he had a powerful wish to be back in his bedroom at home, with all his systems humming and the door securely shut—back where any problem could be solved with a few lines of good code.

He got out his laptop. Its battery was still pretty well charged up. And maybe since he was in an actual city he could even get online. He gave it a try. Yes! He was on. There must be a node nearby.

He checked his e-mail. He had two messages. One was this:

Dear M. Pringle,

We appreciate your interest in our revolutionary vehicle powered by air. Many of very brilliant people are helping develop this car. It is a new adventure most exciting!

Thank you for writing to us, and good fortune on your journey.

The Team

• • •

Duff was thrilled with this message. He could tell by the oddities in the sentences that it was written by actual French people and came from actual France. The M. before Pringle must stand for Monsieur. He liked that—Monsieur Pringle. There was something friendly and exuberant about this note that made him happy.

The second message was this:

Dear Duff,

A minor problem has come up. Looks like expected funding may not materialize. But not to worry!! Worst case, we make the Vortex team a little smaller. Or cut it down to just YOU!!! Know you could handle it!!!!
Ping

Duff wasn't sure what to make of this. Should he be worried or flattered? What exactly was involved in running an entire project? Would he have to do things like budgets and marketing? Would he have to do the work of four or five people?

Moony dashed up to him and dropped the tennis

ball on his keyboard, where it rolled over the keys, leaving a path of dog spit. "He's giving you a turn to throw the ball for him," Bonnie said.

"Oh," said Duff. "Okay." With his thumb and one finger, he picked up the slimy ball. He threw it as far as he could, and Moony bounded away.

"What are you doing?" Bonnie said. She seemed to have got over being mad.

"Getting my e-mail," Duff said. "This one's from the company I'm going to work for."

Bonnie leaned over and peered at the screen. One of her ponytails brushed Duff's chin. "Huh," she said. "So you mean you can get e-mail out of the air? No wires?"

Duff explained about his wireless card, which could pick up signals from receivers installed on phone poles and rooftops in most cities.

"Cool," said Bonnie. "And can you go on the Web, too? Like could we get to the Hairy Oatmeal website right from here?"

"Sure," Duff said. He proceeded to demonstrate. They checked out Hairy Oatmeal, Plastic Rayguns,

CruddPile, Elevator Music, and a few more of Bonnie's favorite bands. Duff navigated with swift, practiced fingers, pausing only to throw the slimy tennis ball for Moony every couple of minutes.

He felt a pressure to be interesting, to make up for having been clumsy before. He said, "It's like you have a probe out to the entire universe. You can find out anything. Just ask a question and you get an answer. Usually. Or you get twenty thousand answers, sometimes, which is not necessarily useful, because then how do you find the one that's really, you know, the one you . . . unless your search engine is optimized for . . ." Why was he saying all this? He was getting tangled up in his words. She was probably thinking, Total nerd, get me out of here.

"Okay," she said, "then if we can ask anything, let's ask it what's happened to Stu."

Duff glanced at her to see if she was kidding. She was. He tried again.

"I found something *really* amazing yesterday," he said. "A car that runs on air."

"Oh, sure," Bonnie said.

"Really. No gas at all, just air. Want to see it?"

Bonnie shrugged. "Okay."

Duff brought up the website he'd found yesterday. He read the article out loud.

"We ought to have one of those," Bonnie said, but she seemed distracted. She stood up. "Stu must have got kidnapped. It's after seven o'clock." Then, after a moment, she said, "Uh-oh," and started walking away.

Duff looked up. Over by the picnic tables, he saw Moony, who had his paws up on a bench beside a fat guy in a backward baseball cap. A second later, Moony jumped up on the bench and snatched something from the table. The fat guy started yelling, and Bonnie ran toward him. She scooped up Moony, said something to the fat guy, and the fat guy, in a loud voice and with many hand gestures, said something to her. Then she turned around and came back to Duff.

"Moony ate his deviled egg," she said. "Boy, was that guy mad. My fault. I have to keep an eye on this dog. He runs off." She put Moony back in his carrying case and closed the door.

"*Okay*," she said, and her tone of voice made Duff snap his eyes up from the screen. "We have to do something. Stu's been gone an hour and a half. You stay here with our stuff, and I'm going to go look for him."

She walked off before Duff could even answer. He watched her go. She marched across the lawn, her arms slicing back and forth, her hands curled almost into fists. Nobody better get in *her* way, Duff thought.

He shut down his laptop and zipped it into its case. He should have been the one to go out looking for Stu. He should have said, in a take-charge way, "Enough of this waiting around," and ventured out into the streets of Amarillo. But oh, no. He was glued to the computer screen, as usual. He plunked down onto his duffel bag, put his elbows on his knees and his chin in his hands, and gazed at Bonnie's retreating back, now just a white spot at the edge of a street at the far end of the park. She was waiting for a red light to change. When it did, she sprang forward, running. Why running all of a sudden? Duff stood up and shaded his eyes with his hand. The white spot that was Bonnie ran toward a red spot on the other side of the street. Both spots stood still for a moment facing each other, their arms moving, and then they came back in Duff's direction.

It was Stu, of course. Bonnie had found him right away, or he had found her. They came closer, growing from spots into people again, and when they came up to him, Duff said, trying but failing to keep the irritation out of his voice, "So how come it took you an hour and a half to buy cigarettes?"

"Time got away from me." Stu shook his head, smiling ruefully. "The fascinations of beautiful downtown Amarillo, man. I just kind of lost myself in 'em."

Should have lost yourself permanently, Duff thought.

"And listen," said Stu. "I got talking to a few locals, and it sounds to me like we should get off the freeways and take the scenic route to Albuquerque. There's a lot of great stuff to see in this part of the country! We'd probably avoid a lot of traffic, too. And instead of staying here tonight, we ought to get out into the desert, find a campground, and sleep under the stars. Much better than some dump of a motel, and a lot cheaper. Doesn't that sound terrific?"

Duff and Bonnie answered simultaneously.

"I don't know," said Duff.

"I'd love to," said Bonnie.

"Great!" said Stu. "Let's get going."

Chapter 11
DUFF FALLS IN LOVE

Stu drove. Once they got outside Amarillo, he drove at a furious speed, zooming along the highway much faster than you'd expect from someone who'd expressed an interest in scenery. Bonnie sat in front, and Duff sat in back next to Moony's carrying case. A little way outside the city, they passed a famous attraction—the Stanley Marsh Cadillac Ranch, a line of ten Cadillacs stuck nose first in the ground, as if they'd crash-landed there from a drive through the sky. Stu didn't want to stop and look at them. "It's a total waste," he said. "Those great old cars buried! Old Stanley must have been nuts."

After that, the scenery was flat and boring. Every now and then, Duff saw a ball of twigs rolling across the ground. A tumbleweed, he decided.

Stu seemed to relax after a while. He slowed down, and he and Bonnie started joking around. "This is UFO territory," said Stu. "They like these big, flat, empty places. Easier to land."

"I hope one lands near us," said Bonnie. "I've always wanted to see an alien."

"That's easy," said Stu. "We've got one right in the backseat."

Bonnie turned around and grinned at Duff. "But he isn't green," she said.

"No, but he's definitely from another planet."

Duff's bad mood intensified. He was going to have to get himself away from Stu. Stu seemed to bring out the worst in him. Around Stu, he was jealous, irritable, and defensive, and he felt both superior (in brain power) and inferior (in coolness). Also, something about Stu was very fishy, and Duff didn't want to be associated with it, whatever it was. The trouble was, how could he get away from Stu without leaving Bonnie, too? In fact, how could he get away from Stu at all, since he had no car to get away in?

At least, though, he could stop pretending that he thought Stu was just a nice innocent guy. He was going to have to get some truth out of Stu. Like why did he disappear like that back in Amarillo? Why was he suddenly so keen on taking the scenic route? For his own self-respect, he was going to have to ask these questions, though he disliked confrontations so much that even the thought of one threatened to bring on a headache.

There was a sudden hoarse hacking sound: *Kaaagh! Kaaagh! Kaaagh!* Engine failure, was Duff's first thought, but he quickly realized the sound was right next to him. Moony was standing up in his crate, his spine arching, his head stretched forward, his mouth gaping. Uh-oh, thought Duff. He scooched away, but not soon enough. The contents of Moony's stomach shot through the wire mesh of the crate and landed half on the car seat and half on Duff's leg.

"Yeeuugh!" cried Duff.

Bonnie whipped around. "Oh, Moony! Oh, poor thing. Stop, Stu." Stu pulled over. Duff thought "poor thing" should really apply to him as much as Moony, but he helped Bonnie clean up the mess. Stu just sat, drumming his fingers on the steering wheel.

"Moony should ride in the front for a while," Bonnie said. "Being in the backseat might be making him carsick." So they put Moony's case on the front seat and Bonnie climbed in the back next to Duff. "Of course, it might also be that deviled egg he ate," she said.

"Then put him in the back again," said Stu, "and *you* sit up here."

"That's all right," Bonnie said. "He deserves to ride in the front for a while. He hasn't had a turn this whole way."

Sitting next to Bonnie turned out to be a little disturbing for Duff. Sometimes when the car took a sharp turn her arm pressed for a moment against his arm. Since he had on a short-sleeved T-shirt and she had on a tank top, it was actually skin pressing against skin. Bonnie didn't seem to notice this at all, but Duff found himself wishing this road through the desert had turns at more frequent intervals.

Duff didn't notice any campgrounds along the road. He didn't see much of anything, in fact, except dry earth and a few scrubby bushes. They'd been driving for over an hour, and it was nearly dark. Where were they going to sleep? Cramped into the car? Stretched out on the ground?

He could see that Bonnie was getting worried, too. "There's *nothing* out here," she said. "I'm starving. Where are we going to eat?"

"Don't worry," Stu said. But he didn't offer any solutions.

More miles went by. More stretches of desert, more twiggy bushes, a few leaning-over wire fences. Not only were there no restaurants or towns or campgrounds out here, there were hardly any cars. They hadn't seen even one for at least half an hour. "Hey," said Stu, "if we don't see a good place to stop, we'll just drive all night." But his voice lacked the usual jauntiness.

More miles, more desert. Darkness everywhere. And then, in the beam of the headlights, a sign at the side of the road. Stu slowed down. It was a hand-made sign, a board about two feet long standing on two poles, with these words painted in artistic yellow letters outlined in orange: SUNLIGHT VILLAGE, ½ MILE. Beneath the words was an arrow pointing up a dirt road that led off to the right.

"Aha!" cried Stu. "Problem solved."

Well, maybe, thought Duff. But he was relieved. Whatever Sunlight Village was, it couldn't be worse than sleeping in the car. Or driving all night.

The road was awful—deep ruts on either side of a weedy hump down the middle. Stu drove it so fast that Duff and Bonnie bounced around in the back-seat like marbles in a can, and Moony's crate banged against the dashboard. But in five minutes, they were arriving in Sunlight Village.

It was a collection of small mudbrick houses, with paths winding among them. Light glowed from their windows. Various ancient vehicles stood here and there. They drove until they came to a kind of plaza more or less in the center of the village. On a plot of straggly grass stood several large rectangular panels of glass, each about the height of a person, propped up at an angle, like big flat faces gazing at the sky.

"Is that art?" said Stu.

"I don't know," said Duff.

Two people were walking toward them through the warm night—a big man with a black mustache and beard, and a floaty-haired woman in a long green sundress and sandals. A black Lab, its feet brown with dust, trotted along after them.

"Greetings," said the man, stooping down to speak to Stu through the car window. His face, what you could see of it behind the hair, was friendly. "What can I do for you?"

They all got out of the car, and Stu turned on the charm. He introduced the three of them. They were sort of lost, he said, on their way west, had been hoping to find a campground, but . . . He smiled and shrugged and looked hopefully at the bearded man.

"You're welcome here," the man said. "We're always happy to take in travelers. I'm Jasper. This is Star."

"So what is this place?" Bonnie asked him. She took Moony's case out of the car and set it on the ground. Moony and the black Lab sniffed at each other through the wire mesh. "Sort of a commune?"

"A community," said Star. Duff noticed that she wore star-shaped earrings and a blue and gold star on a chain around her neck. Probably her real name was Barbara or Jane or something. "Jasper and I and a few others founded it fourteen years ago. We wanted to leave behind the false promise of material possessions and live simply in harmony with the Earth."

"Oh," said Duff.

"Very fine," said Stu. "Way to go."

"What are these things?" asked Bonnie, pointing to the glass panels standing on the lawn. "Are they meant to be, like, spiritual?"

"No," said Jasper. "They're photovoltaic panels. The sun shines on them and turns into electricity. That's our power plant."

Duff stared at the glass rectangles. He'd heard of getting electricity from the sun, but he'd never seen it in action. Did these panels—there were eight of them—run the whole village? What happened on cloudy days? What happened at night? He was about to ask these questions, but Star was leading them on toward a large building with a covered walkway across the front, where some dusty-footed children were playing with a cat. "This is our meeting hall," said Star. "It's our dining room, too. Down at that end is our guest room. You boys can put your stuff in there. Bonnie, you and your puppy come with me. I have a spare bed at my house. We've had our dinner already, but I'll bring out the leftovers for you."

The guest room was next to the kitchen, at the far end of the meeting hall. There were four beds in it, and between the beds were bamboo screens that stood about six feet high, so you could make yourself a little private space. Duff and Stu chose beds at opposite ends of the room. There appeared to be no other guests.

At dinner they sat in a big room full of long tables, where the residents of Sunlight Village were talking and laughing over their after-dinner tea. Star brought out dishes of unfamiliar foods accompanied by brown rice. There was a reddish stew that seemed to be made of peppers, a greenish gravy over pale spongy lumps, and a bowl of something smooth and orangish that might have been pumpkin or sweet potatoes. Duff ate a lot of everything—whatever it was, it tasted good—and he noticed that Stu and Bonnie did, too. "Better eat up while you can," Bonnie said. "My aunt Shirley basically lives on cottage cheese." She reached for another hunk of butter-soaked cornbread.

This brought back to Duff's mind the whole purpose of his journey, which was starting to slip his mind. "How long does it take to drive from Albuquerque to Los Angeles?" he asked.

"I don't know," Bonnie said. "Probably a long time."

Duff ran through his schedule calculation again. Today was Friday, June 28. He'd get to Albuquerque tomorrow, Saturday, the twenty-ninth. But how was he going to get from there to San Jose by Monday morning? By car—even if he had a car—there just wasn't enough time. He was going to have to take a plane after all. How much would a one-way plane ticket cost? Did he have enough left in his account? He didn't know. Even if he did, he'd arrive in San Jose pretty much penniless.

All around them, the residents of Sunlight Village were having lively conversations. Star was talking about the vegetable garden, where the fourteen zucchini plants were coming along well. "I've found so many great recipes for them," she said. "This year we'll have zucchini bread, zucchini soup, zucchini pudding, and stuffed zucchini. And let's see, zucchini leather, curried zucchini, sweet-and-sour zucchini, zucchini chutney . . ." Someone else was going on about a jammed-up tractor engine, and down at the end of the table, Duff heard bits of a conversation about beetles in the potato patch. But what he wanted to know about were those big glass panels.

When he'd eaten as much as he could, he excused himself and went out to look at them again. There was just enough light in the starry sky to glimmer on the polished surface of the panels. He could see that silver wires ran beneath the glass, making an elegant crisscross pattern. The panels didn't hum or buzz—they were perfectly silent. It was beautiful, he thought—the vast bowl of the desert sky overhead, strewn with stars, and down here the windows glowing with soft yellow lamplight, produced by sunbeams that had fallen on these panels during the day.

It was so beautiful, in fact, and so ingenious, that

Duff fell in love with the whole idea. These people had power without noise, without oil, without stink, without even paying for fuel. Why weren't these panels all over the country? Why weren't they running office buildings and cities and cars? Did they come in different sizes? Could you hook a little one up to your computer? Could a car have one of these on its roof and—

"Hey!" called a voice. "Duffer! Get in here!" It was Stu, beckoning from the doorway of the meeting hall. "Bonnie's going to sing," he said. "Hurry up."

Duff hurried. Inside, people had gathered down at one end of the room, where Bonnie was taking her guitar out of its case. She plugged its cord into an outlet in the wall (a sun-powered electric guitar, Duff thought) and perched on the edge of a table.

Duff was standing next to Star, who said, "I adore music. Every morning, I sing my song to the sunrise. It's an ancient Pawnee chant."

"Uh-huh," said Duff, though he wasn't really listening. He was too busy watching Bonnie, who looked quite different tonight. Her hair wasn't in a ponytail or pigtails. It fell straight down beside her face, covering her ears, curving forward at the ends. Her guitar was the flat shiny kind with a sort of horn at the top. She plucked a string, and a bright twangy note flew out. She twisted a key, plucked again. Was she nervous? She didn't look it. She almost looked unaware of all the people watching her.

She bent her head, and her hair fell across her face. Then she looked up and flashed a smile at her audience. "I'll sing you this one I wrote myself," she said. "It's called 'Lost Dog.'"

She looked up at the ceiling for a second, as if maybe the words were printed there—and then her fingers ripped across the guitar strings, her head jerked back, her eyes closed, and out of her mouth came the strongest, wildest, most heart-wrenching voice Duff had ever heard.

Duff was thunderstruck. Some door he hadn't known existed opened up right in his deep middle, and Bonnie's voice blasted through it, scorching everything that was in there. For the second time within ten minutes, Duff fell in love. How could he be all shaken up by a girl wailing about a lost dog? But he was. He was.

Chapter 12
STRANDED

Duff couldn't sleep that night. He lay on the guest room bed, listening to Stu's boring breathing, wishing he knew how to make Stu disappear. He wasn't surprised that Bonnie liked Stu better than him. Stu was cool. Duff was not so cool. Stu had an easy way of talking and joking; Duff did not. But he was smarter than Stu, wasn't he? And he was a good person. Why wouldn't a girl go for a good person, instead of someone shifty like Stu, who was probably a runaway and maybe something worse?

Duff wanted a chance to prove how smart and good he was. If he could just show it to her somehow, maybe she would take notice of him. Scenes arose in his mind in which he did wonderful things while Bonnie happened to be watching. The trouble with these scenes was that the wonderful thing he did was always very vague. In the scene, he had just done it, whatever it was, and Bonnie was full of wonder and admiration, and she was saying how she'd never understood before what an amazing person he was, and he was saying it was really not much, and she was putting a hand on his arm and looking up at him and . . .

When he wasn't thinking about Bonnie, he was thinking about Stu. Now that it was night, when everything seems more fraught with peril than in the daytime, getting the truth out of Stu felt dangerous. What if Stu was one of those people who seemed normal most of the time, but when threatened went into a psychotic frenzy and attacked? Or what if Stu was completely innocent after all, and Duff ended up feeling like an idiot for accusing him?

All this interpersonal stuff was so horribly hard. He had no built-in program for it, the way other people seemed to. All he could do was blunder through it and hope not to look like too much of a fool.

In the morning, having slept a total of what felt like fourteen minutes, Duff got up as quietly as he could, dressed, and went outside. Star was standing on the east side of the courtyard with both hands lifted above her head, singing something in a high, tremulous voice—her Pawnee chant, Duff guessed. The first rays of the sun were hitting the glass panels, and now Duff could see that they were a beautiful deep blue. Jasper was tinkering with something in back of one of them. Duff went over to him.

"How do these things work?" he said.

"Well, I don't know the technical details," said Jasper. "But in some way the panels take the energy of sunlight and convert it into electricity, and then the electricity runs down this wire"—he pointed to a wire that ran from the foot of the panel into the ground— "to the batteries that are in that shed over there. The batteries store the electricity, so we have power not just in the daytime, but at night, too, and on cloudy days."

"I like it," said Duff.

"Yep, we like it, too."

"So why aren't there more of these around? Like in cities?"

Jasper shook his head. "This technology's not ready to take over the world yet. To power a city, you'd have to have acres and acres of these. Thousands of 'em."

"Could you run a car on them?"

"It's been done. The trouble is, the batteries are so heavy. Someone's got to make a big technological leap before we can get power really efficiently from the sun." He went back to his task, tightening a screw on the stand that held the panel. "Where are you heading today?"

"Albuquerque," said Duff. "Bonnie's aunt lives there."

"That Bonnie can sing," said Jasper.

"Yeah," said Duff. "She's not bad."

• • •

After breakfast (granola for the human beings, dog food plus a few scoops of last night's dinner for the dogs), they said their good-byes to Jasper and Star and loaded their things into the trunk of the car. Duff got into the driver's seat. He started up the ignition. The engine made a sluggish, groaning sound: *graaugh, graaugh*. It paused. It made the sound again. A bolt of fear shot through Duff.

"Engine's just cold," said Stu. "Try again."

He tried again. After a few more *graaugh*s, the engine caught, to Duff's extreme relief.

Stu was clearly relieved, too. "Good going," he said. "Sunlight Village is an interesting place to visit, but we probably don't want to spend the summer here. Think of all the zucchini we'd have to eat."

Bonnie sat in the front passenger seat with Moony on her lap. He seemed to be over his stomach troubles. For the next two hours, he slept soundly, except for little spasms of dreaming, during which he made yippity noises and his paws twitched. Stu dozed in the backseat.

The scenery on the way to Albuquerque was mostly

desert, though there were some hazy mountains to the north. The sun blazed down. The inside of the car heated up, and opening the windows only made it windier, not cooler. By eleven o'clock, they all felt like wilted spinach. "We'll stop and get something to drink," Duff said. They had hooked up with the free-way again at a place called Tucumcari and were no longer out in the middle of nowhere. Duff pulled off at a likely-looking exit, and they found a gas station. Here they filled the car's tank, and they all bought sodas from the vending machine.

"Okay," Duff said when they were back in the car. "Just an hour or so to Albuquerque."

He turned the key. *Gra-a-aaugh*, said the car's engine, in an even more sluggish way than before. How could the engine still be cold in this heat? He turned the key again. This time the engine was silent. "Well," he said in his most confident voice. "Good thing we're at a gas station. Whatever's wrong with it they can fix."

But they couldn't, as it turned out. It was Saturday;

the mechanic didn't work on weekends. Stu opened the hood and poked around inside, but he couldn't tell what was wrong, and besides, he said, it was too hot for working on engines. "What do we do, then?" said Duff.

Stu shrugged. "I'll think of something," he said, but there was an unfamiliar note of doubt in his voice.

Phone Call #5

Saturday, June 29, 2:48 PM

Rosalie: Hello?

Burl: Hey, it's us.

Rosalie: Where are you?

Burl: Albuquerque. Four seventy-eight Cactus Wren
Way. But they aren't here.

Rosalie: They aren't? How do you know?

Burl: No Chevy outside. Also we rang the doorbell.
No answer.

Rosalie: They'll show up. You just got ahead of them
somehow. Sit in the car and wait.

Burl: How long? It's hot here.

Rosalie: Don't complain. Ten percent, remember.
Call me again if they still aren't there by
tomorrow.

Burl: *Tomorrow?* But what're we gonna—

[Click.]

Chapter 13
AUNT SHIRLEY TO THE RESCUE

It was Bonnie who came up with the solution.
"I'll call my aunt. She'll come and pick us up, and on
Monday they can fix the car and she can drive Stu
back to get it." She made the call from a phone
booth behind the Dumpster. It took her quite a
while. Duff watched her pace back and forth as she
talked and waved her hand in the air. Finally she
hung up and walked back to them. "She'll come,"
she said. "She doesn't love it, but she will."

For the next hour and a half, they sat on a tiny

patch of grass over by the gas station restrooms, shaded by a scrawny bush, and tried not to expire from the heat. Duff's thoughts swirled around in a limp, random way. Project Rapid Vortex, Bonnie's singing voice, photovoltaics, french fries—they all bobbed up, but he didn't have the energy to pursue any of them. His shirt was sticking to his back. Sweat dripped into his eyes.

At last a big, blunt-nosed van, cherry red, pulled up at the station. It stopped, its huge door opened, and out stepped a small, wiry woman with white blond hair arranged sculpturally on her head. She wore ironed jeans, a pink silk blouse, and glittery earrings in the shape of hearts. Duff and Stu and Bonnie hauled themselves up off the ground and went to meet her. Bonnie gave her a peck on the cheek.

"This is my aunt, Shirley Hopgood," Bonnie said. "Also known as LaDonna Wildmoor."

An alias? thought Duff. She's a criminal, too?

"My pen name," said the aunt. "I'm a writer."

Oh.

"It's great of you to come and get us," said Stu.

Shirley gave him a narrow-eyed look. "And you are?"

"Stu Sturvich," said Stu. "Volunteer driver for your lovely niece. On my way to pursue interests in California. Also"—he waved a hand at Duff—"Duff Pringle, computer genius."

"And how do you happen to know Bonnie?" Shirley asked, looking at Duff.

Duff started to explain about his job in Silicon Valley, and his car that broke down, and how he'd met Carl and driven the Chevy to St. Louis, but long before he was finished Shirley nodded briskly and said, "I see, I see," and told them to put their baggage in the car because she had things to do and couldn't stand here talking in the blazing sun. "What is this?" she said when Bonnie lifted Moony's carrying case into the back.

"This is Moony," Bonnie said. "My dog."

"Oh, dear," said Aunt Shirley.

When the van was loaded, they climbed in. Bonnie

sat in the front, Duff and Stu sat in back, and Moony sat in his crate in the space behind them. Aunt Shirley drove at a good clip down the road, and even faster when they got to the highway. She would zoom up in back of a car, ride its rear bumper for a minute or so, as if threatening to drive right over it, and then ram her delicate foot down on the accelerator and pass the car in one great swoop. This made for a rather lurching ride for the passengers, who didn't have a steering wheel to hold on to, but Aunt Shirley didn't seem to notice. She was busy talking.

"I don't believe anyone would call me a critical person," she said. "But I must say, Bonnie, that I am the tiniest bit annoyed with my sister. This is the fourth time this has happened. If she has to engage in illegal activities, why can't she do it more intelligently?"

"I don't know," said Bonnie.

"I'm amazed you can tolerate it."

Bonnie shrugged.

"Well, never mind. I don't like to be negative. Let's

talk about you, dear. I haven't seen you for quite a while. What are you up to?"

"Oh, school, you know. And singing."

"Singing? In the school choir? How lovely. That's interesting to me, dear, because in my latest work I have a musical theme, a soprano who falls in love with the orchestra director, a man who has vowed never to marry again after the tragic death of his first wife in a volcanic eruption."

"Actually, I don't sing at school, I sing with my guitar," said Bonnie. "I write my own songs."

"Oh, pop music? I see. Well, that's lovely, too. I often mention a sweet popular tune in my writing, as a sort of background music. Do you know 'Your Bluebell Eyes'? Or 'Be Still, My Naughty Heart'?"

"I write my own songs," Bonnie said again. "I don't know those." She turned away and gazed out the window.

Aunt Shirley, who was thundering up behind a VW, didn't ask what kinds of songs Bonnie wrote. "I find that weaving a strand of music through my stories is deeply enhancing," she said. "Though of course in the movies it's much easier, you can have real music." She passed the VW by swerving into the slow lane, causing Duff to crash sideways into Stu. "I'm confident that movies will be made of my books before long. The only obstacle is my agent, who simply will not push hard enough."

Listening to this conversation, Duff felt bad for Bonnie. She not only had a criminal for a mother but a conceited airhead for an aunt. He gazed at the back of Bonnie's neck, trying to beam sympathy at her. He could see the backs of her ears and the little gold stems of her earrings. The label of her T-shirt was sticking up. He thought about reaching forward and tucking it back down. Would it be all right to do that? Would she be freaked out? Should he say something casual first, like, "Your label is sticking up, I'll fix it for you"? Or should he just do it? After thinking about it this way for several minutes, he decided that because it was impossible to do it in any way that seemed natural, he'd better not.

Outside, the landscape was filling up with houses. The closer they got to Albuquerque, the more trucks roared alongside them, huge trucks trailing gray smoke from their exhaust pipes. There were also a lot of old pickups and old jeeps and old panel trucks, also trailing smoke. "Look at all that," Duff said. It made him grumpy. "How come those guys aren't arrested for pollution? They're messing up the atmosphere even worse than we did in the Chevy."

"Oh, gripe, gripe," said Stu. "Mr. Pollution-Buster." He reached over and tucked down the label at the back of Bonnie's T-shirt. "Label's sticking up," he said. Duff felt hatred like a lake of boiling oil around his heart.

Around four, they pulled into the driveway of a Spanish-style house with a neat green lawn and a pink potted geranium on either side of the front door. The automatic garage door yawned open, revealing a garage that already contained a car, a much smaller car than the cherry red van. A blue Toyota, Duff saw as they pulled in. He also noticed a battered black car parked across the street, which caught his attention because there were two men sitting in it—not starting up the car or getting out of it, just sitting there. He and Stu and Bonnie unloaded their bags, and as they did, the two men stared at them. Odd, Duff thought.

They went into the house. Moony had to stay in the garage, inside his crate. "My decor is unsuitable for dogs," Shirley said. "It's pastel." The door from the garage led into a very neat kitchen. A bowl of artificial daisies was exactly centered on a round table, and a row of spotless copper pots hung above the stove. From the kitchen, Duff could see into the living room, where the carpet was pale rose, the curtains were looped and fringed, and glass animals stood on spindly tables. This was the sort of house a large, tall person would have to move carefully in—or, even better, not go into at all.

But here he was, and here he would be for one night at least, until he could come up with transportation for the next leg of the trip. If somehow he could make it to Los Angeles by tomorrow, then maybe he could get to San Jose the next day—the very day he was supposed to start work. How he would do this he didn't know.

Phone Call #6
Saturday, June 29, 4:20 PM

Rosalie: Yes.

Rolf: Us. They just got here—Bonnie, two boys, and Shirley. In Shirley's car.

Rosalie: What? *Shirley's* car?

Rolf: Yeah. No Chevy.

Rosalie: [Furious sputtering]

Rolf: What should we do?

Rosalie: Get in there! Ask Bonnie! Ask her where my car is! And ask her who those punks are she's got with her, too.

Rolf: Okay. Will do.

Chapter 14
CRASHING AND SAVING

Aunt Shirley vanished into the back of the house, saying she had to get right to work, and Duff and Stu and Bonnie stayed in the kitchen to see if there was anything to eat. Bonnie foraged in the refrigerator and came up with some fruit salad, some lettuce, some raisin bread, and some nonfat yogurt, and they made a small, unsatisfactory snack of that. No one talked much. Duff found himself staring at Bonnie's hand, which was holding a piece of raisin bread. Her fingers were so slim and tender-looking he didn't see how they could get those ferocious sounds out of the guitar. She wore rings on three of her fingers—silver rings with stones in them of different colors. He watched her hand carrying the bread up to her mouth and down again, up to her mouth and down, and then he watched her lips moving around as she chewed, until finally Bonnie said, "Do I have lettuce stuck in my teeth or what?"

"No, no," Duff said. "Sorry. I'm just thinking."

"About what?"

"Well, I want to get to Los Angeles tomorrow. I don't know how I'm going to do it."

"I don't know either," said Bonnie.

"Or me," said Stu. "I've gotta get to San Diego."

"Hitch," said Bonnie.

"I guess," said Stu.

"And you, too," said Bonnie to Duff.

Duff just nodded. Stu wiped the last of his bread around his plate, mopping up the yogurt. "I was wondering," he said. "That car in the garage, the blue Toyota. Is that your aunt's, too?"

"Yeah, that's her car from before she bought the SUV. I think she's going to sell it."

"Is that right?" Stu inched his chair closer to the table and leaned toward Bonnie. "Do you think she'd sell it to me?"

"I don't know. You could ask her."

"I will do that," said Stu. He drummed his fingers happily on the table.

Duff said, "You have enough money to buy a car?"

"Well, depending what she wants for it," said Stu. "Even if it took all I had, it would be okay. Once I get to San Diego, I can stay with my buddy till I get a job. Think I could go out and take a look at that car?"

Bonnie shrugged. "I guess so."

"I'd just like to know what kind of shape it's in, you know, just check it out. This way?" Stu opened a door that led from the kitchen to the garage and went through it. Duff heard the clack of a latch and the skreek of the car's hood being raised.

He was now alone with Bonnie. Here was his chance to say something that would get her attention, but what that was he didn't know, because all the words he had ever learned in his life deserted him the moment Stu left the room. Bonnie was wiping off the table with a sponge. He watched her hand move back and forth. He thought of saying, "You have a nice hand," but didn't. He thought of saying something about her singing, but what?

And then he thought, Am I going to be like this forever? A slave to shyness? Tortured by fear? No. He couldn't stand it. He refused. A dizzy, reckless feeling flared up in him. He opened his mouth, willing to risk the worst. And—magically, it seemed—words came. "Your singing last night," he said. "It was pretty great."

Bonnie stopped, with the bread wrapper in one hand and the yogurt carton in the other. "Really? You thought so?"

"I did," said Duff. Now that he'd spoken, he found he could keep going. "You've got . . ." He searched for the right word. "You've got *passion* in your voice."

Bonnie smiled, a crooked little embarrassed smile. "Wow," she said. "Thanks."

Metallic tapping noises came from the garage. Duff thought about what to say next. "How'd you get into singing?" he asked after a moment.

Bonnie stuffed the bread wrapper into the yogurt carton and sat down at the table again. "It was because of my mom, in a way. Practically the only good thing she ever did for me. Mainly she goes back and forth between ignoring me and then paying a lot of attention to me because she feels guilty for ignoring me. In her paying-attention phase, she gives me presents. Most of them I hate. But when I was twelve she gave me this guitar that she got from a pawn shop, and I taught myself to play it."

"That's kind of like me," Duff said. "This kid I knew in fifth grade, his parents gave him a new computer and he gave me his old one. I learned it on my own."

Bonnie smiled. "And so you got passionate about computing, right?"

"Well, yeah, I did. That's how I am, I get intense about things. A *few* things. When I was a little kid, it was space aliens, and then computers, and just on this trip I've gotten kind of fascinated by, you know, other kinds of energy like french fry oil and that sunlight electricity, and then—" He stopped. He'd been about to go right on and say how the next thing he'd gotten passionate about was her. Yipes. He'd shut his mouth just in time.

"And then what?" said Bonnie, but he didn't have to answer that question, because the doorbell rang.

From the rear of the house Aunt Shirley called, "Somebody! Please! I'm trying to concentrate!"

Bonnie got up, and Duff followed, curious. When she opened the door, he recognized the two men outside as the ones who'd been sitting in the car across the street. Bonnie obviously recognized them, too.

"What are *you* guys doing here?" she said.

"Your mom sent us," said one of the men. He was short and muscular, with a jowly face like a bulldog's. "She's worried about you. Wants to make sure you're okay."

"I'm fine," said Bonnie. She didn't ask them in.

"And she was wondering who you're traveling with,"

said the other man. He was younger and skinnier. He had a fuzz of blond hair on a head shaped kind of like a light bulb.

"Two guys I met," said Bonnie. "They've been great to me." She stepped back. "Tell her everything is fine, Rolf." She started to close the door.

"One more thing," said Burl, the bulldog guy. "Where's her car?"

"Oh, the car." Bonnie told them where it was and said she'd be picking it up on Monday.

"Your mom wants it back," said Burl.

"Why? It's not like she's going to be needing it."

"She wants it safe in her driveway. She was very clear about that." Both Rolf and Burl nodded.

Bonnie shrugged. "Okay. I don't need it. *You* pick it up, then. You can pay for the repairs and take it home. I don't care."

Big smiles broke across both guys' faces. Talking at the same time, they said, "Fine, great, glad you're okay, kiddo, see you later," and then they turned around and headed across the street to their little black car.

Bonnie closed the door. She was about to say something to Duff when a shriek of rage sounded from the back of the house. Somewhere up a hall, a door was flung open. Rapid steps approached. And then Aunt Shirley appeared in the living room, her face bunched up in fury.

"It's happened again! I can't stand it. Cannot, cannot stand it."

"Stand what?" said Bonnie.

"This freezing and crashing! Six times already this week it's done it. And I had just written the most thrilling passage! Which is lost, of course, I'll never be able to re-create it." She staggered into the kitchen and sank onto a chair. "Maybe it's time for me to go back to writing by hand, as I used to. My fountain pen never did this to me."

Duff cleared his throat. "If you like," he said, "I could take a look at it for you."

"You may if you want," said Aunt Shirley, "though I'm afraid it's going to take someone who really knows what he's doing to fix it."

"He *does* know what he's doing," said Bonnie. "He's a computer genius."

"Last time this happened," said Aunt Shirley, "I had a whole team here from Lizard Computer, and it took them hours. And as you can see, they only fixed it temporarily."

A possibility was occurring to Duff, a thrilling possibility. He was being handed the chance he'd wanted to do something wonderful—and without Stu around to mess it up. Here it was, the very thing he knew best in the world. His heart started up a little rappety-rap in his chest. "I'm pretty sure," he said, "I could fix it for you in about fifteen minutes."

"Really?" Aunt Shirley raised her slim eyebrows. "Well, no harm in trying. Come this way."

Duff turned to Bonnie and said, "You come, too, all right? I might need, um, help."

Bonnie shrugged and followed. On the way down the hall, she told Shirley that some friends of her mother's had come to take the Chevy back to St. Louis, and she wouldn't have to drive out and pick it up from the gas station after all. "Good," said Shirley. "I have enough problems without *that*."

So they were friends of her mother's, Duff thought. No wonder they looked like thugs.

The studio of LaDonna Wildmoor was neat and organized and mainly pink. The walls were pink, the carpet was pink, and the covers of the books lined up on the shelves seemed to be mostly pink, too. The computer on the desk was gray, but it had been decorated with pink stickers shaped like hearts. On the screen was a message saying "Error #889bxj54. Source code unknown." Other than the message, the screen was blank.

All right. If Duff had been wearing long sleeves, he would have rolled them up. He tried to organize his thoughts. But his thoughts resisted being organized, because of Bonnie. She had draped herself over a long lounge chair in the corner, leaning back on the pink pillows, and settled herself to watch. Duff felt like a magician about to do an elaborate trick.

Focus, focus, he told himself. He sat down in front of the computer. All right: Why is this thing crashing?

Software conflicts, most likely. He restarted the computer. While it was coming up, he asked Aunt Shirley questions. What operating system was she running? What word processing application did she use? What version? What other stuff? To most of these questions she didn't know the answer. "I don't deal with the technical," she said. "My realm is the creative."

"This is pretty boring so far," said Bonnie from the chaise.

"I need to download some programs," said Duff. "Can we go online?"

Aunt Shirley typed in her screen name and password, and then Duff zoomed around in cyberspace, finding version 2.03 of this and version 3.1 of that. While they downloaded, he waited awkwardly, wishing he knew the sort of patter that magicians use between tricks. Aunt Shirley, fortunately, filled in the silence.

"It was so good, that last paragraph, the one that's lost. I'll never remember it. Something like, 'Her eyes, those hyacinthine eyes, held secrets his heart yearned to know . . . ' No, it wasn't yearned, it was more like 'held secrets that called to his heart from a distant place . . .'"

Duff thought, as he installed the conflict detection program on Aunt Shirley's hard disk, that he wasn't sure what color Bonnie's eyes were. Maybe hyacinthine? Or were they sort of aqua? He was consumed with a sudden desire to know. But he didn't turn around. "Now," he said, "I'll run the conflict detection program." He did so. Checked the results. "Looks like you need an upgrade to a couple of your applications," he said. "I'll just pull those down for you." He was moving fast, talking casual, aiming to give an impression of effortless mastery.

"See?" said Bonnie. "I told you he knows what he's doing."

Duff smiled. This was going well.

"Are you sure you can't get that paragraph back?" said Aunt Shirley. "It was one of my most lovely passages."

"If you didn't save it, it's gone," said Duff. "But I'm sure you have many beautiful passages in you."

He flicked from one website to another. "While I'm

at it," he said, "I'll get you a little bonus item—like a thank-you present for giving us a ride." A nice audio player, maybe, for her romantic music. Or an interesting screensaver. He found a site with lots of choices— flowers, fish, spiders, kittens, cupids, swirling fractals in neon colors.

A hand settled lightly on his shoulder. Bonnie leaned down to look at the screen and spoke close to his ear. "Oooh, those are cool," she said. "Get her one of those."

And Duff almost lost it. A bolt of lightning went through him, his hand got unsteady, and instead of clicking the Heart-and-Cupid screensaver, he clicked the Tarantula Army screensaver, and hordes of hairy spiders began crawling across Shirley's monitor.

Shirley shrieked.

"Wait a sec," Duff said. "No problem, I just—"

"I knew it!" Shirley cried. "I never should have let you *touch* my computer!"

"Calm down," said Bonnie. "It's just a little—"

"What does it mean? What does it mean?" screamed Shirley. "Is everything lost?"

"No, no," said Duff, frantically maneuvering. He was so flustered he couldn't get the blasted spiders off the screen. Bonnie was still peering over his shoulder. He could feel her breathing on his neck.

Shirley grabbed his arm and pulled. "Get away from there!" she cried. "Get away before you do anything worse! I'm calling Lizard right now!"

Bonnie gripped Shirley's belt and yanked on it to get her away from Duff. "Let him fix it!" she said. "Leave him alone!"

In another second, Duff would have been tipped out of his chair onto the floor and probably clawed to shreds by Shirley's long pink fingernails. But just as he was about to lose his balance, he managed to make the spiders disappear. Shirley let go of him. Quickly, he clicked the Heart-and-Cupid screensaver, and when the rosy little cupids appeared, floating back and forth across the monitor, Shirley started breathing normally again. "Oh," she said. "Well, that's rather nice. And is my chapter still there?"

"Certainly," said Duff. "All but the part you hadn't saved when the system went down."

"See?" said Bonnie. "I told you he could do it."

"And the crashing problem," Duff said. "I fixed that, too. You shouldn't have any more trouble."

"Well, thank you," said Shirley. "I'm sorry I got a little upset. I'm severely arachnophobic."

"You're welcome," said Duff. Bonnie was smiling at him. A warm, humming feeling came over him, as if the pinkness of the room had seeped into his veins and was making him glow.

Then footsteps sounded in the hall, and a moment later, Stu appeared in the doorway. "Hey, everybody," he said, "what's happening?" No one answered, so he carried on. "Ms. Hopgood, can I ask you a question? It's about your car."

Chapter 15
THE THIRD CAR

"Yes?" said Aunt Shirley. She was already sitting at her computer, bringing up her almost-lost chapter. She didn't turn to look at Stu, so he went around to the side and spoke to her profile.

"You know your car? The Toyota? Bonnie says you're selling it."

Aunt Shirley nodded, intent on the screen.

"So what I wondered is, how much are you asking? 'Cause I'd like to buy it."

When Duff heard this, two feelings arose in him at

almost the same time. One was hope. If Stu bought that car, then he, Duff, had a way to get to California. Immediately following was shame: he had vowed to have nothing more to do with Stu from here on. Would he betray his conscience for a ride? He was afraid he might.

"Four thousand," said Aunt Shirley.

Two more feelings surfaced in Duff: disappointment (Stu couldn't possibly pay that much) and relief (he wouldn't be tempted to betray his conscience after all).

"Okay," said Stu. "If I give you cash, could you make it thirty-five hundred?"

And then came the strongest feeling of all: astonishment. Stu had thirty-five hundred in *cash*? Followed by suspicion: where did he get it?

Duff glanced at Bonnie. She met his eyes for an instant and gave a tiny shrug of her shoulders. She was mystified, too.

But Aunt Shirley was ready to seize the deal. Stu went to get the money out of his backpack, and when he came back, they carried out the transaction right there in her office. Duff watched in amazement as Stu counted out a stack of big-number bills, and Aunt Shirley took the pink slip out of her file cabinet and signed it over to him. "This saves me the trouble of advertising," she said. "Really, both you boys have been so helpful."

For a moment, a very good feeling and a very bad feeling fought for control in Duff. The battle was so equal that they canceled each other out. He stood there in the pink office feeling blank and stunned.

By then it was dinnertime. Aunt Shirley showed her appreciation by cooking up a meal: spaghetti with low-fat mushroom sauce, iceberg lettuce with low-fat ranch dressing, and white bread spread with a low-fat butter-like substance. How could a person live on stuff like this? Duff wondered. Though he'd eaten hardly anything all day, he didn't have much appetite, not only because of the food, but because the stunned feeling had gone away and his mind was in turmoil. Once again, his conscience was ordering him to confront Stu. He didn't want to. He wanted to ride quietly with

Stu to Los Angeles and there say good-bye to him for-ever. But he couldn't. That wad of bills had pushed things over the line. Stu was up to something, and Duff couldn't just let it slide.

So after dinner, while Bonnie did the dishes and Shirley went back to her office, Duff said to Stu, "Come outside with me for a minute and let's make a plan."

They went into Aunt Shirley's backyard, where lawn chairs with flowered cushions sat on a concrete terrace beside a turquoise swimming pool. The sun was disappearing in a haze behind the house.

"Listen," said Duff. He was nervous but determined. "I have to talk to you about something."

"Okay," Stu said. "What?"

"Come over here." Duff led Stu around to the other side of the pool, away from the open windows of the house. "I have to ask you this," he said, "because . . . I just do."

"Ask away," said Stu.

Duff braced himself for the possible psychotic

break. He took a deep breath. "First of all: What really happened in Amarillo? When you disappeared like that?"

Stu looked into the glimmering swimming pool water. He looked up at the sunset. Then he said, "I spotted someone I used to know. Wow, was I surprised! A guy from Florida. So I went after him. And we hung out for a while, talking."

"I don't buy it," said Duff. "Give me the truth." He was surprised to hear himself sounding so tough. Maybe that moment in the kitchen with Bonnie, when he'd managed to just say no to fear, had activated a whole new subroutine of his personality program.

"Hey, watch it, man." Stu scowled. "Are you saying I'm a liar?"

"I am," said Duff firmly. "And if you don't tell me the truth, I'll tell Aunt Shirley you're an escaped convict on the run, and that the money you gave her for the car was stolen loot."

Stu frowned at the diving board for several seconds. He frowned down at his feet, dusty in their sandals.

Then he said, "Okay, listen, it's nothing so terrible. You remember I mentioned about how my parents wanted me to join the military? And how I was in a little bit of trouble?"

"Yes," Duff said.

"Well, the trouble was, I borrowed a guy's car. Just for a little ride, you know? It was kind of a valuable car. And accidentally I banged it up some. It wasn't my fault! Some idiot in front of me made a left turn from the right-hand lane. But the guy was pretty mad."

"The guy who owned the car?"

"Right. He happened to be kind of a big shot. Big freakin' businessman in town, and kind of fanatic about his cars. He wanted me to get a job and pay for it, which would have taken like a hundred years. My parents were pushing me to join the military and make a man out of myself. I didn't like those options, so I left. I gotta have *freedom*, man!"

"So what does that have to do with disappearing in Amarillo?"

"I saw a guy in the park and I thought it was him.

Looked just like him. I was sure he'd come searching for me. So I got out of there as fast as I could. Spent some time exploring the back alleys of the Amarillo shopping district."

"And that's why we took the scenic route to Albuquerque?"

"Right." Stu grinned his big-toothed grin and held his hands out to his sides, palms facing the sky, the picture of innocence now that he'd confessed. "That's it," he said. "You're not going to turn me in, are you? And send me back to a life of torture and misery?"

"I have another question," Duff said, pressing on. "What about that money?"

"What about it?" Stu asked.

"Where did you get it? Hitchhiking surfers don't usually go around with big wads of cash in their pockets."

"None of your business," said Stu. He smiled, but Duff could see a little quiver at the corner of his mouth.

"All right," said Duff. "I'm calling Shirley." He turned toward the house and took a few steps. But before he got far, Stu grabbed his arm.

"Okay, okay, listen," he said. "I found that money. I *found* it, okay? Finders keepers, right?"

"Found it where?" said Duff.

"In the Chevy," said Stu. "I was just looking over the car, you know? Checking it out. Such a great car. Happened to look under the floor of the trunk and hey. There it was."

"How much was there?"

"A lot."

"How much?"

"Well, I haven't had time to count every bit. More than twenty thousand, though."

"But it isn't yours."

"Whose is it, then? Huh? Bonnie's mom's?" Stu stretched his head forward and skewered Duff with his eyes. Duff took a step back, being careful not to fall in the pool. "That was stolen money, man. That money belongs to me just as much as it does to her."

"It does not," said Duff. "It belongs to whoever she stole it from. The police ought to have it, not you. I ought to call them right this minute." Duff held on to his new tough-guy style, but he was feeling uncertain. If he did call the cops, he'd have to prove somehow that Stu stole the money. Aunt Shirley would probably get hysterical, and Bonnie might get in trouble. Also, he'd have to sit on Stu or tie him up to keep him from running off before the cops arrived. It all sounded complicated. And on top of everything, he'd be left without his ride to Los Angeles.

These thoughts ran through his mind in a few nanoseconds and produced, to his surprise, an idea. "Or," he said, "I could make you a deal."

"What deal?" Stu squinched up his eyes suspiciously.

"You drive me to Los Angeles. You sell the car. You send the money—*all* of it—back to Bonnie. She can do whatever she thinks is right."

Stu thought about this, pursing his mouth and tilting his head to the side. Finally, he said, "Okay. It's a deal." He sighed. "You know, man, I'm not really into crime. I mean, not in a big way. I saw that money in there, and what could I do? There wasn't any reason *not* to take it. The only person who knew it was there wouldn't be needing it. Even if it *was* hers, which it wasn't." Stu kicked off his sandals and sat down at the edge of the pool. He dunked his feet in the water and kept talking. "I thought, well, with this kind of cash I can even do a little good to make up for the evil way it was gotten. Give some to homeless folks, maybe. Stuff like that."

He looked up hopefully at Duff, who was standing next to him. He wants me to tell him it's all okay, Duff thought. And he's a great guy and everything is forgiven. Well, I'm not going to.

"I didn't like carrying around that much cash anyhow," Stu said, flicking one foot upward so that glistening blobs of water flew into the air. "Made me nervous. Fine with me to unload it on Bonnie." He grinned at Duff. "So off to LA in the morning, huh?"

"Right," said Duff, keeping his face stern. "We'll start early. Seven o'clock."

"Okeydoke," said Stu.

Duff left him there by the pool and went back into the house, where he plunked himself down on a couch with a view of the backyard. He was going to keep his eye on Stu if he had to stay awake all night to do it. The worst thing he could think of would be to wake up in the morning and find that Stu and the Toyota and the money had all vanished into the burning Southwest air.

The rest of the evening started out really well. Bonnie didn't exactly sing, but she sat on the floor and strummed her guitar and hummed, which was almost as good. Stu swam in the pool for a long time, back and forth, back and forth, jerking his head to flip wet coils of hair out of his eyes every time he came up for air. Duff sat on the couch, listening to Bonnie, keeping an eye on Stu, and leafing through a romance magazine he found on the coffee table. It amazed him that some people actually liked these kinds of stories, where women with raven black hair or golden curls were always melting into the arms of men with names like Thorn and Drake. Every now and then he read some especially corny lines out loud, and Bonnie laughed.

Duff felt relaxed and contented. What a great day it had been! So many problems solved—the car problem, the Stu problem, the problem with Shirley's computer, the problem of being too shy to talk to Bonnie. Even, probably, the problem of getting to his new job by Monday. He was incredibly pleased with himself. Everything was going to be fine. The only not-fine thing was that in the morning he and Stu would travel on alone, leaving Bonnie behind. But somehow, Duff figured, he would find a way to see her again.

After a while, Aunt Shirley came into the room. She stood behind the couch silently until Bonnie stopped strumming and Duff looked up from the magazine. Then she smiled a chilly smile. "I really can't have this," she said.

"Have what?" Bonnie asked.

"This distracting environment," said Aunt Shirley. "All this splashing and humming and talking." She closed her eyes and shook her head, a tight little vibration as if this situation were giving her the shudders. "I need silence for concentration," she said.

"But it's after eight," said Bonnie. "Aren't you finished working for the day?"

"My fault," said Aunt Shirley. "I haven't yet told you my schedule, which you'll need to know. I get up at eight, work from nine to two, nap from two to four, do my swimmercizing from four to five, eat dinner at six, and work from seven to ten. So you see"—she smiled again, thinly—"I really do require continuous quiet."

"Oh," said Bonnie.

"Since I've been interrupted anyhow," Shirley said, "why don't I take the opportunity to tell you a little more about how we do things here. I can see that you don't remember." She sat down on a lavender-colored armchair. Duff noticed that she placed her feet neatly together. She was wearing high heels made of transparent plastic, decorated with small daisies. Her toenails were pink. "First of all, quiet, as I've said. Second, tidiness. Everything has its place. No sweaters draped over chairs, no shoes left on the floor, no litter lying around. I really cannot operate in a mess." She held up two fingers and looked at them. "Quiet. Tidiness. What else? Ah. Helpfulness. Of course I won't be charging you anything to stay here, Bonnie. You're a relative! I'd never do that. But I will expect some assistance around the house. Some cooking. Dishes, naturally. Laundry. Vacuuming. That sort of thing. It's summer, after all, so you won't have schoolwork. Let's see. Anything else?" She cast her eyes toward the ceiling. "Well, no dogs in the house, of course. How long were you thinking of staying, dear?"

"Actually," said Bonnie, "I guess I didn't make it clear." She set her guitar carefully back in its case, closed the lid, and flipped the three latches. "I'm not actually going to be *staying* except for tonight. I'm actually going on to Los Angeles with Duff and Stu."

Duff's heart did a high-jump. She's coming with us! Wow, wow! He had a feeling, from the way she'd said "actually" three times, that she'd just decided this in the last minute. What a great decision! It would make everything easier and more fun. And obviously she couldn't stay with Shirley. No point in her mother and herself *both* being in jail.

Shirley looked surprised but not disappointed. "You're leaving tomorrow?" she said. "I didn't realize. When you asked if you could come and stay, I thought— Well." She smiled, and this time it was a nice wide smile, very real-looking. "That will be a lovely adventure. You'll stay with Amelia, then? In her funny little arrangement?"

"Yes," said Bonnie. "That's what I'll do."

At that moment, the sliding glass door opened, and Stu stepped into the living room. Water dripped from his shorts. His wet feet made footprints on the carpet. "Great pool!" he said. He shook his head vigorously, like a dog, and his hair whipped around, flinging droplets.

"PLEASE!" shrieked Shirley, springing up from her chair. *"Not in here!"* She ran at him with her hands out. Stu staggered backward, blundered into a lawn chair, and flopped down on it so hard that it tipped over and pitched him onto the concrete, where he sprawled like a beached octopus while Shirley stood over him shouting about puddles on carpets and people who must have been brought up in pigsties.

Bonnie laughed—one short snort and then a helpless giggle. Duff laughed, too. Laughter boiled up out of him like bubbles out of a shaken soda can, and once he started, he couldn't stop. He doubled over and held on to his stomach. Bonnie laughed so hard she could hardly breathe. Tears rolled down her face. They were still laughing when Shirley came in, having banished Stu to the poolside cabana to change back into his clothes.

"You think it's funny," Shirley said.

Duff and Bonnie tried to look serious.

"What if it were *your* valuable pastel rose carpet?"

Duff made a choking sound at the idea of ever having a valuable pastel rose carpet. Bonnie snorted again and pressed her lips tight together.

"I give up," said Shirley. "I'm much too upset to work. Bonnie, you know where the guest room is. You boys may spread your sleeping bags outside on the lawn."

Duff checked his e-mail one more time that night before going to bed. He found this message:

Dear Mr. Duffy Pringle,

This is to let you know that Ping Crocker is no longer with Incredibility, Inc., and that the company will be ceasing to do business as of June 30. We regret that we must withdraw our offer of employment. We wish you the best of luck finding employment elsewhere.

Yours sincerely,

Beverly Winthrop

Executive Assistant

Duff stared at these words as if they were in a foreign language. He read them again. They seemed to be saying his job was gone. How could this be?

He gazed out at the backyard, where Stu was laying his sleeping bag on the grass. Suddenly, the vision of the future he'd been holding in his mind—himself in a cubicle, writing code and making money, himself in a nice apartment with a swimming pool, himself rising to greatness in the entertainment software industry—was replaced by a giant blank. It was like stepping off a ladder, expecting your foot to touch the ground, and plummeting into a void instead. Duff was so shocked that he felt nothing. He simply sat there on Shirley's couch with his mouth half open. He sat like that for a long time.

Finally, he shut down his laptop and went outside. As he rolled out his sleeping bag, Stu mumbled a few words at him and then conked out completely and started to snore. Duff's stunned mind was functioning just well enough to come up with an idea that would let him get some sleep and keep watch on Stu at the same time. It was tricky, but he thought he could do it. He unraveled a long thread from an inside seam of his shirt, and—very, very carefully, so as not to wake Stu by tickling him—he threaded one end of it through the loop of Stu's earring and tied the other end to his own little finger. That way if Stu tried to sneak out in the night, Duff would know it as soon as he moved.

Then Duff lay down on top of his sleeping bag—it was too warm to get inside—and stared up at the star-dotted sky. The shock of losing his job before he'd even started it was beginning to wear off, and a few feelings were making their way through the numbness. One was anger—he'd been tossed aside like a piece of trash. Another was terror, because he didn't know what would happen next. And still another, totally unexpected, was a wisp of relief, a sense that the closing down of this door might somehow lead to the opening of others.

Phone Call #7

Sunday, June 30, 7:15 AM

Rosalie: What.

Rolf: We got the car.

Rosalie: Good. So get on the road.

Rolf: We didn't find any money in it.

Rosalie: Look harder. It's under the floor of the trunk.

Rolf: We looked there. We looked everywhere.

No money.

Rosalie: [Deadly silence.]

Rolf: I said, No money.

Rosalie: I heard you. One of *them* must have found

it. You have to go get it.

Rolf: But what if they—but how do we—

Rosalie: That's your problem. Just do it.

Chapter 16
THE CHASE

By seven fifteen the next morning, they were on the road. The Toyota wasn't as spacious as the old Chevy, and it smelled a little like perfume, but it ran all right, and that was all that mattered. Duff was in the driver's seat this morning, with Stu beside him and Bonnie and Moony in the back.

Aunt Shirley had given them a breakfast of artificial eggs, white toast, and grapefruit juice, and then she'd hustled them out into the garage, waved as they backed the Toyota out, and turned to go into the house.

"Wait!" Duff called through the window. "Where's the freeway from here?"

"That way," said Shirley, pointing to the right. "Call when you get there, Bonnie," she said, and she flapped her hand once or twice. Then she stepped back into the kitchen and closed the door.

So Duff was now making his way to the right, through a maze of streets. Residential streets at first— rows of stucco houses, most of them with red-tile roofs. Then came commercial streets, lined with used-car lots, video stores, taco stands, gas stations, stores selling rubber swimming pools, Navajo rugs, cut-rate mattresses, plumbing supplies. Morning traffic made for slow going. Finally, up ahead, he spotted a sign for Interstate 40.

Outside the city, the land stretched reddish and treeless on both sides of the road, dotted with scrubby bushes and rising here and there into sudden rocky ridges and flat-topped hills. The sky was immense and blue—an exhilarating sight. "Okay!" he said. "This is marathon day! Less than eight hundred miles to Los Angeles. We'll be there by tonight."

Stu settled in. He turned on the radio, put his feet up on the dashboard, and opened the window just enough to riffle the hair on the top of his head. "Can't wait," he said. "Kind of sad, though. We'll be splitting up when we get there."

"Don't forget to give me the name of that friend," said Bonnie from the backseat.

"Friend?"

"The one in the music business."

"Oh, yeah. Just remind me later. I'll write it down for you."

Uh-huh, thought Duff. He had now decided that hardly anything Stu said was true.

After a few minutes, Stu took his feet off the dashboard and twisted around to talk to Bonnie. He went on about the music world for a while and then started in on the surfing world—the beaches he'd heard of, the famous surfers he hoped to meet, the spectacular runs and wipeouts he himself had experienced. Duff tuned him out. He focused on the road, two lanes of blacktop in each direction, separated by a strip of bare ground. He hadn't told anyone yet that his job had evaporated. Best to keep it to himself, he thought, until he had an alternative plan. He'd work on a plan while he drove.

But a change in Stu's tone startled him out of his thoughts.

"Hey!" Stu exclaimed. He was looking through the rear window. "That guy back there is really riding our tail. And it looks like he's waving at us. What's up with him?"

Duff glanced in the rearview mirror. Sure enough, right behind them, so close it looked like it was about to ram into the trunk, was a black car. A familiar-looking black car, with two familiar-looking people in it, one of them waving frantically.

A horn honked—not just a friendly beep, but a long, loud blast.

"What's their *problem*?" cried Stu.

Bonnie twisted around to look. "That's Rolf and Burl!" she cried. "Following us!"

Bonnie was right—the driver and his passenger were

the two guys who'd come to Aunt Shirley's door. "Why would they be following us?" Duff said.

"I don't know!" said Bonnie.

"I don't get it!" said Stu. "What's happening? Who's Rolfen Burl?"

"It's Rolf *and* Burl," said Bonnie. "Two of them. They work with my mom. They came to get the Chevy, don't you remember?"

"He was in the garage," said Duff.

"What did they want with the Chevy?" Stu asked.

"My mom wanted it back. Urgently."

There was a brief pause. "Oh," said Stu.

The horned blared again. Duff looked in the rearview mirror and saw Burl jabbing his finger toward the side of the road. "They want us to pull over," he said.

Bonnie leaned forward, gripping the back of Stu's seat. "They were going to drive the Chevy back to St. Louis," she said. "So how come they're following *us*?"

"They have a bad sense of direction?" said Stu. He was facing forward now, hunkering down low in his seat.

"No," Bonnie said. "It must be because of me. My mom must have told them to come after me for some reason. But why would she? She doesn't want me home. I don't understand it."

Duff understood it. Those guys had been sent to bring the *money* home, not Bonnie. They hadn't found the money, so they were coming to get it.

He sped up. He passed a big tanker truck to his left and moved over into the fast lane. In the rearview mirror, he saw the black car change into the fast lane, too, and pull up close behind them again. He didn't like this. These guys were outlaws. They might do anything. Duff felt his neck and shoulders stiffening, as if to fend off a bullet.

It was hard to think while he was driving fast and weaving in and out of traffic and fearing for his life, but he figured out this much: If Rolf and Burl managed to stop them, they'd find the money on Stu. They'd either keep it for Rosalie when she got out of jail, or they'd steal it for themselves. Either way, the bad guys would get it. Therefore, Duff concluded, as he stepped hard on the gas and streaked past a tour bus, he'd do his best to *keep* them from getting it. That way it would end up in Bonnie's hands and maybe eventually in the hands of the people who'd been bilked out of it in the first place.

Stu craned around and looked out the back window again. "They're gaining on us, man," he said. "Speed up."

Duff was already going nearly eighty. He had a terrible suspicion that Aunt Shirley's old Toyota wasn't happy at that speed. He could feel a tremor in the car's skeleton. But he pressed on the gas just a little harder anyhow. He thought of car chase scenes he'd seen in movies, where the bad guys zoomed up beside the good guys and then edged over until either the good guys drove off the side of the road or crashed. That would be bad. But having your car shake itself to pieces when it hit ninety would be bad, too. Trickles of sweat ran down Duff's ribs. He swerved into the slow lane, just ahead of a pickup with a horse trailer.

A blurping sound came from the backseat, followed by a revolting smell. "Moony!" cried Bonnie. "Oh, poor baby, he's carsick again!"

"Aargh," said Stu. "That's all we need." He opened his window, letting in a rush of air.

"All over his cushion," said Bonnie. "Yuck."

Duff had a sudden memory flash: Was it just last night he'd decided his problems were solved and everything would be easy from here on in? How wrong a person could be, he thought. How quickly the universe could turn on you.

"But wait a second!" said Bonnie. "How do they even know I'm here? I didn't decide to come till last night!"

"Must have gone back to Shirley's and asked," Duff said. Letting Bonnie think she was their target was easier, for now, than explaining about the money.

"Come on, man, hurry up," said Stu, who was peering into the side-view mirror. "Those guys are trying to come up beside us."

Duff put on a desperate burst of speed, but it wasn't enough. The black car, now in the fast lane, pulled up even with them, and the passenger-side window went down. The lightbulb face of Rolf appeared. He yelled something at them.

"I don't like this," said Stu. He scrunched down in his seat. "Are those guys gangsters or what? Do they have guns?"

Bonnie rolled down her window and screamed at Rolf. "Get away from us! Get away!"

Instead, the black car edged closer.

"They're trying to push us off the road!" Bonnie cried. "Go faster, go faster!"

"I can't!" said Duff. He already had the accelerator to the floor. "Anyhow, we can't go ninety all the way to Los Angeles! We've got to get off the highway and lose them."

"Good idea," said Stu.

"All right!" said Bonnie. "Next exit."

They sped along neck and neck with the black car for another harrowing few minutes, Rolf shouting and waving his fist at them the whole time, Burl inching the car dangerously close to theirs, Duff inching away dangerously close to the edge of the highway, until finally a green exit sign appeared.

Duff veered off the highway. The black car, caught by surprise, rocketed onward in the fast lane, and for a second Duff thought they were safe.

But Bonnie, who was now kneeling on the seat looking out the rear window, shouted, "Oh, no! They're coming back!" And Duff saw in the rearview mirror that the black car had cut across the lanes, stopped with a squeal of brakes on the shoulder of the highway and was now racing backward to the exit, spraying gravel from its wheels. By the time they'd gone a few hundred yards down the road, Rolf and Burl were on their tail again.

Duff had hoped to come to a town, where he could somehow zigzag around in the streets and confuse his pursuers. But he saw no sign of civilization. The road they were now on cut across the same barren landscape they'd been passing through all morning—dry earth, scrubby bushes, rocky hills. No cars, no people. And Rolf and Burl barreling up behind them.

"We have to stop!" he said. "Or they'll make us crash."

"Up there!" Stu cried. He was pointing ahead and to the left. "It's a restaurant or something! Pull in there! There'll be people! These guys won't shoot us down in front of people!"

Duff saw a small white building in the distance. He headed for it. "As soon as I stop," he shouted, "we all get out and run inside!"

He veered off the blacktop onto a rocky road, bumped along it, and screeched to a stop in the restaurant parking lot, which was empty except for weeds. All three of them jumped out of the car, and as soon as they did, they saw their mistake: this restaurant was not open for business. Its windows were boarded up. Its door was padlocked, and grafitti covered its walls.

A second later, the black car roared up behind theirs and halted. The doors opened. Rolf and Burl got out.

"Now you listen to me!" yelled Burl, striding up to them. He was breathing hard. He pointed a finger (not a gun, Duff saw with relief) straight at Duff's face. "You punks took something that didn't belong to you and we've come to get it."

"I'm not going back!" Bonnie shouted. She grabbed onto Duff's arm on one side and Stu's on the other. "You can't make me! I'll turn you in for kidnapping!"

Burl blinked at her. "Not you," he said. "We're not after *you*."

"You're not?" Duff felt Bonnie's grip loosen. "Then what? Then what the heck have you been chasing us for?"

"You know," said Rolf. He glared at Stu.

"We do *not*!" said Stu in a voice of such wounded innocence that Duff forgot for a second that he was lying. "You chase us all over the freeway, you scare the crap out of us, and *we have no idea what's going on*!"

Rolf and Burl both stared at him. Duff could almost hear their minds grinding slowly, trying to decide what to do next. Finally Burl said, "Nice try, kid. You won't give it to us, we'll find it ourselves. Empty your pockets, all of you."

Well, all right, thought Duff. Change of plan. Money goes back to crimeland instead of to Bonnie. Nothing I can do about it now.

"Fine!" said Stu furiously. "Fine, search anywhere you want! Whatever you're looking for, you won't find it."

Duff almost had to admire his bold defiance. He must know that his stash of cash was about to be discovered.

"I don't get this!" cried Bonnie. "What right do you have to—"

"Just do it!" said Rolf. His voice was high and shrill, like a knife slicing the air.

So they all turned their pockets inside out. Nickels and pennies, lint-covered cough drops, some key chains, a jackknife, a couple of barrettes, and a bunch of other small stuff fell to the cracked asphalt. Rolf and Burl thumbed through their wallets, patted them down, and found nothing of interest. They moved on to the car. "Open the trunk," said Rolf.

Here we go, Duff thought. He opened the trunk, where their backpacks were stowed. Rolf started tossing things out of the trunk, unzipping packs, rifling through them, flinging T-shirts and underwear onto the ground. He looked in Bonnie's guitar case and her purse. Burl got in the front seat and rummaged through the glove compartment, scattering maps. He looked under the floor mats and under the seats. He pushed his hand down between the cushions. Finding nothing, he moved on to the backseat.

"Get this dog out of here," he said. "It stinks."

"Oh, Moony!" Bonnie ran to the car and hauled out his case. "How could I forget you?"

"Check the dog's crate," said Rolf.

Burl opened the crate door and pulled Moony out with one hand and the cushion with the other. "There's barf on everything!" he said. He felt around in the crate, shoved Moony and his soggy cushion back in, and then, making gagging noises, grabbed one of the T-shirts on the ground to wipe his hand.

Duff watched with growing amazement as Rolf and Burl just about took the car apart—pried off the hub-caps, wrenched the interior panels off the doors, unscrewed the headlights, even looked in the engine. Any minute, he expected one of them to come up with a thick packet of bills, wave it in their faces, and speed away. But the only halfway interesting thing they found was an old crumpled sheet of paper on which was typed "*Scarlet Desires*, by LaDonna Wildmoor."

What did Stu *do* with that money, Duff wondered, swallow it?

"See? *See?*" Bonnie said. "There's nothing!"

"Now, look." Rolf aimed an evil look at her. "There was a real valuable item in that Chevy when it left St. Louis, and last night it wasn't there. How do you explain that?"

A perfect answer to this question flashed into Duff's mind. "It's obvious," he said. "Someone at that gas station found it. Whatever it was," he added.

"Absolutely right!" Stu chimed in. "That's gotta be it. And you've just driven a hundred miles and freaked out some innocent young people for nothing."

Rolf and Burl looked at each other. A spark of doubt passed between them.

Bonnie took advantage of it. "Is my mother ever going to be mad at *you*," she said, "when I tell her you almost killed us."

Burl wavered. . . . Duff could see uncertainty in his eyes. But then he pressed his mouth into a tight grim line. "Take your shoes off," he said.

"Our *shoes*!" Bonnie yelled. "That is *too much*! I can't *believe*—"

But both Burl and Rolf came at them in such a menacing way, as if about to rip their feet off, that they all bent over, undid their laces, kicked away their shoes, and peeled off their socks. "Check 'em," ordered Burl.

Rolf peered into all the shoes. He turned all the socks inside out. Nothing was there but lint.

This was apparently the last straw. Rolf did some creative swearing, and Burl turned on him with a furious look. "Shut up," he said. "You're driving this time."

Without another word, they turned around and got back in their little black car. Rolf started the engine and stepped hard on the gas. The tires spun on the asphalt, throwing up scraps of weed, and the car took off down the bumpy road and headed for the highway.

As soon as it disappeared, Duff and Bonnie and Stu all shrieked and whooped and (as soon as they'd put their shoes back on) jumped around, joyful for their different reasons. Stu picked up rocks and threw them in the air, Bonnie let Moony out of his case, held him by his icky front paws, and danced with him, and Duff ran three times around the abandoned restaurant to get the tension out of his muscles.

Then they picked their stuff up off the ground and put it back in the trunk. Stu replaced the hubcaps Rolf and Burl had pried off, and he put back the inside panels of the doors as well as possible, given that they were kind of torn up. In just over half an hour, they were on their way again.

Stu drove. He put the window down and hot wind rushed in. "WOOHOO!" he shouted. "Good guys win, bad guys lose!"

Duff sneaked a sideways glance at him. Without turning his head, Stu grinned. It was a gloating grin, the grin of a person who clearly considered himself not just a good guy, but a really smart good guy.

"I still don't understand what they were looking for," said Bonnie from the backseat, where she was wiping off Moony's paws with a rag she'd found in the trunk. "It wouldn't be drugs. My mom isn't into drugs at all. I don't think she is, anyway."

"Maybe she is," said Stu. "Yeah. That must be it. That would explain the whole thing."

Chapter 17
TRUCK STOP

They drove along merrily past endless vistas of scrub brush, tumbleweed, and flat-topped mountains. Stu was in such high spirits that he started singing without even turning the radio on, and he and Bonnie sang loud, out-of-tune versions of one song after another, Bonnie doing the high parts and Stu making twangy, strummy noises to imitate the guitar parts. Duff looked out the window at the scenery. Now that they were headed for California and would (barring any further disasters) actually *be* in California sometime that night, he had to face the great blank abyss of his future. He tried to picture something that would fill up that blank, but nothing came to him. His mind was as empty as the landscape.

They had crossed the border into Arizona. The country became more dramatic. Ridges of reddish rock slanted up out of the ground. Pine trees started to appear on hills.

Stu and Bonnie had stopped singing now. Everyone was quiet. They'd been up since six o'clock and had been through a lot since then. They were tired. They passed a sign on the highway for something called Petrified Forest National Park, and Stu said halfheartedly, "We ought to go see that," but no one answered and he didn't turn.

After a while, Stu said, "Anybody hungry?" It was just after one o'clock by then.

"Starving," said Bonnie.

"Me, too," said Duff.

"I saw a sign for a truck stop café," Stu said.

"That's where the best food always is, at truck stops. Want to try it?"

They did want to, and so a few miles farther on, Stu took an exit off the highway and drove up to a little restaurant with about a hundred huge trucks in the parking lot, many of them with their motors rumbling and their exhaust pipes puffing and gasping. They were like a herd of enormous animals at a watering hole.

"Perfect," said Stu. He parked the car. "I'm gonna change into a better shirt. This one's all sweaty from our little episode of terror."

Bonnie took Moony out of his crate and put his leash on. "I'll walk him around a little bit," she said. "Poor baby."

Stu got his backpack out of the trunk. He tossed the car keys to Duff and said he'd take the barf-stained cushion with him to the men's room and clean it off. Duff walked with Bonnie and Moony around the edge of the parking lot, where Moony lunged eagerly at sandwich crusts and bits of french fries and peed on various rocks and bushes and truck tires.

Inside, the restaurant was crowded with truckers and also with tourists—dads studying maps, moms mopping up spilled drinks, kids yelling and wailing and dropping food on the floor. The restaurant was plain but pleasant, with big windows, and booths with red plaid seats. It smelled like a weird mixture of hamburgers and air freshener. Bonnie and Duff got one of the few empty tables, and the waitress gave them menus. Just the sight of all the different things on the menu made Duff feel suddenly almost faint with hunger. No wonder, he thought, remembering how small and pale his last two meals at Aunt Shirley's had been.

"Trucker's Delight," Bonnie read. "That sounds good."

"Or what about the Long-Haul Burrito?" said Duff, scanning the choices. "Or the Tanker Sandwich?"

"Yeah," said Bonnie, laughing. "Real food!"

"I don't know how your aunt Shirley survives on what she eats," Duff said.

"I don't, either. She wants to keep herself all small and neat and perfect. Her whole life is small and neat and perfect." Bonnie's smile faded. She put her menu down and frowned at it. "She's so different from my mom. I think my mom has a much better imagination than Aunt Shirley. *She* ought to be the writer. She'd probably be a better writer than a con artist."

It seemed risky to say anything about Bonnie's mother, seeing how Bonnie had reacted to Duff's clumsy attempts at sympathy before. So he said nothing. He looked out the window, where a couple of trucks were heading out of the parking lot, groaning and puffing.

Bonnie didn't say anything for several seconds. Then, in a husky voice, she said, "I'm sorry for snapping at you the other day in the park. I can't stand it when people are nice to me about my mom, because it makes me want to cry, and I hate crying. I hate for anyone to *see* me crying. Like that day in the backyard."

"Well, yeah, I sort of figured that out," Duff said. "That you've had a rough time, having your mom be . . . gone so much."

"I hate it. You just can't imagine how much I hate it."

"I bet I can," Duff said.

"No, you can't, not unless you've spent a million hours by yourself waiting for her to come home when she said she would. Or moved constantly from one crummy place to another to keep ahead of the law, so you just get to know people at your school and then you have to leave. My whole life, my mother's had these stupid schemes that she says are going to make us rich. She's wanted all over the place." Bonnie turned to look out the window. "Unlike me," she said.

"Unlike you?"

"I mean, I don't feel exactly *wanted* anywhere." Bonnie picked up her paper napkin and looked down at her lap as she unfolded it.

"Oh," said Duff. Once again, he had no words. But he had a feeling, a strong one: it was an ache of sympathy, a pain somewhere around his heart. Without thinking, he reached out and laid his hand on Bonnie's arm, just for a second or two. She looked up and their eyes met. A slim invisible arrow shot through Duff's chest. Then Bonnie smiled and picked up her glass of ice water. She took a drink, wiped her mouth with the back of her hand, and thumped the glass back down.

"But now," she said, "things are going to be different. This time I'm not going back. I bet Amelia will have me, and if she won't, I'll . . . I'll . . . I'll do something else."

The waitress arrived with her little pad of paper. "Ready to order?" she said.

And only then did Duff realize that Stu had been in the men's room a very long time, even for someone who was washing off a stained dog cushion.

Bonnie must have realized it, too. "Where's Stu?" she said, looking around.

"I don't know," said Duff. "Maybe I should go look for him. You order some food—I'll eat anything."

He made his way among the crowded tables to the back of the restaurant, where a hallway led to the restrooms. He pushed open the men's room door. An elderly man was in there, combing his hair. No one else. On the floor beneath the sink was Moony's cushion, not washed. As soon as Duff saw it, he knew: Stu had split. While he and Bonnie had been talking, Stu had been out in the parking lot catching himself a ride with one of those truckers.

Duff felt strangely calm. He walked out to the parking lot, just in case, by some miracle, Stu was back at the car doing something innocent. But Stu was nowhere to be seen. So Duff returned to the men's room and picked up Moony's cushion. With a wet paper towel, he scrubbed off the worst of the barf. Why hadn't he seen this coming? he asked himself. They'd all been feeling so happy to have escaped Rolf and Burl, and Stu was being friendly and cheerful and offering to help with cleanup and everything—Duff just forgot for a moment about being suspicious. He could have been mad at himself for this, but it seemed useless. Sooner or later, Stu would have found a way to take off.

Duff put the cushion back in the car with Moony

and went back into the restaurant. It was time to tell Bonnie everything, he decided. He plodded over to the table, where Bonnie was sipping on a soda.

"Stuff has happened," he said, sitting down.

Chapter 18
THE WEIRDNESS OF STU

Luckily, they still had the car. Stu could have taken off in it, along with Moony and all their belongings, but he hadn't. That was nice of him. It was typical: as he'd said, he wasn't into crime in a big way, just a small way. He'd lie and steal and betray people and weasel out of things, but he wasn't really *mean*.

So Bonnie and Duff, when they'd finished their lunch, which took a long time because there was so much to talk about, went back out to the car to start on the last lap of the trip. Bonnie brought a big paper cup of water from the restaurant and got Moony as clean as she could. She put him and his pillow back in the crate, and she settled herself in front next to Duff.

It was 2:30. If Duff could hold up as the sole driver, they had a chance of making it to Los Angeles by midnight. The bad thing about this was that it seemed impossible. Duff was already pretty tired, and he could feel a headache waiting to attack him just at the thought of the five hundred miles ahead. The good thing was that it gave him nine hours or so to be with Bonnie, with no Stu to distract her with his flaky promises. Duff's nervousness about talking to her had gone away. Or maybe not exactly gone away but amped up into a kind of excitement that was more thrilling than disabling. It had started when he touched her arm and that one serious look flashed between them, and then it grew as he told her about Stu and why he disappeared in Amarillo and where the money to buy Shirley's Toyota had come from and the deal Duff made with him in

Albuquerque—and Bonnie, instead of calling him an idiot for being taken in, said she thought he'd done the right thing, or at least tried hard to, and she admired him for it. She wasn't very sympathetic about his lost job, though. "That wasn't the right job for you, anyway," she said.

Now, in the car, he felt as if his blood were speeding through his veins. Not only speeding, but had an added ingredient, something fizzy like soda water. His whole body fizzed and hummed. His eyes felt more open, he could feel the roots of his hair tingling. All the right side of him, the side next to Bonnie, was electrically charged. Was this happiness? Was it maybe even love? Maybe it would keep him going during the long hours of driving that lay ahead.

"What I don't understand," said Bonnie, as they sped west out of Flagstaff, "is where he put the money. Do you think he just left it at Shirley's?"

"No," said Duff. "I could tell from the way he looked at me after we got free of Rolf and Burl that he was pleased with himself for outsmarting them. He had that money, but he hid it somewhere they missed."

"Maybe it's still in the car," said Bonnie, "and he went off without it and left it for us to find."

"I think not," said Duff.

"I think not, too," said Bonnie.

They drove along looking out the window for a few minutes. Duff thought it was too bad he was missing all the sights he'd intended to see. Just up north of them was the Grand Canyon, which he'd been looking forward to. He'd have to take another trip some time in the future, a more leisurely one.

After a while, he said, "So tell me about your aunt Amelia."

"She's great. She's an actress."

"Really? Is she famous?"

"Not especially. She does TV ads mostly. She lives by the beach. She has a bulldog named Ernie—Moony will love him. And she's the only sister who hasn't been divorced even once."

"Pretty good. What's her husband's name?"

"Linda. It's a she."

Duff's eyebrows shot up. "Oh," he said. "Hey. That's, um . . . wow. I've never met any gay people."

"I bet you have," Bonnie said. "You just didn't know it."

The car hummed along. Good thing Aunt Shirley had taken care of her Toyota, Duff thought. Another breakdown would be more than he could handle. For this trip, he thought, mentally crossing his fingers, maybe they were through with car trouble.

"The thing is, about that money," said Bonnie, "I never had it—since it wasn't mine—so I don't feel bad about losing it. My *mom* will, but I don't."

"Well, the car is yours," said Duff. "That's something."

"True," said Bonnie. "I'll have to get my license."

"I hope Rolf and Burl aren't beating up the poor guys at the gas station," Duff said. "Maybe I shouldn't have said that about them taking it."

"No, that was good," Bonnie said. "It got them off our backs."

"They must be extremely unhappy about now,"

said Duff. "Having to tell your mom they didn't find the money."

"Serves them right," said Bonnie shortly. "I'm sick of this whole business of schemes and scams. I'm sick of people like them."

"And like Stu," said Duff.

"Stu is weird," said Bonnie. "Sort of a combination of good and terrible. I kind of liked him, actually. He was fun. And I thought he was really going to help me with my career. But he never did tell me that friend's phone number."

"What friend?"

"The friend in the music business. In LA."

"Could be there is no friend," Duff said.

"Probably not," Bonnie said. She sighed. She put the window down a little way and stared out. Wind ruffled her bangs.

"I suppose he's heading for Phoenix," Duff said, "and from there to San Diego."

"He'll probably just keep on running and running," said Bonnie.

Duff nodded. "He has to have freedom. He told me that."

"Yeah, but freedom to do what? To just drift around, mooching off other people and stealing stuff? What's the point of that kind of freedom?"

Duff shrugged. "He's weird."

They contemplated the weirdness of Stu in silence for a while. Not total silence—Moony was moving around restlessly in his crate, scratching and turning the way dogs do when they're readjusting their bedding. Bonnie turned backward to look at him. "He's making a mess," she said. "Pulling the stuffing out of that cushion."

She faced front again. "What will you do when we get to Los Angeles?" she asked. "Now that you don't have a job to go to?"

"Sleep," said Duff, "if your aunt will let me stay the night. Then after that—I don't know. I've been thinking about it."

"What have you thought?"

"Well, programming's what I know how to do. It's

what I like. But maybe I could be a programmer in a different industry."

"Like what industry?"

"Maybe something to do with transportation. Remember that car I showed you on the Web that runs on air?"

"Uh-huh."

"And that bus in Oklahoma City that ran on soybeans?"

"Yeah."

"Well, I don't know, I'm kind of interested in all that. I think it might be better than the entertainment software side of things." In a modest mumble, he told her about wanting to do something important, something that would really change the world. "I might have to go to college," he said. Strangely, college seemed less useless and terrifying than it had before. Duff no longer thought he already knew everything he needed to know. In fact, he had a hunger for learning, now that he had something new to learn about.

"Cool," said Bonnie. "That sounds a whole lot better than making a robot that plays chess, or whatever. I think you're too good for that."

Duff didn't know what to say to this. Heat rushed up into his face.

"I don't mean too good a programmer," Bonnie went on, "I mean too good a person. I could see that you were a good person, after I got past your show-off stuff."

"Show-off stuff?" said Duff weakly.

Bonnie twisted around in her seat to stare straight at him. "Yeah, all that about how much you know, what an expert you are, what a great job you're going to—all that. I get so sick of how boys do that. Like Stu, talking about all the famous people he knows. They think it's going to make girls like them, but it doesn't."

"Oh," said Duff.

"But you want to do something good for the world," said Bonnie. "I admire that. And you said nice things about my singing."

"Your singing," said Duff, "is truly fine. Someone's

going to notice you for sure. I think you'll make it."

"I'm going to try, anyway," Bonnie said. "Even if you and Stu hadn't come along, I was going to get to California somehow. Sooner or later. I was going to hitchhike."

"I'm glad you didn't," said Duff. "Too dangerous."

"I would have been fine," said Bonnie.

"I don't know," said Duff. "Girl hitchhikers always get picked up by serial killers."

"Not always," said Bonnie.

"Once would be enough."

The landscape they were passing through was beautiful, in a strange way, but monotonous. Red rocks. Flat tan earth, little shacks now and then. You didn't feel that you had to keep looking at it or else you'd miss something. So after a while, Bonnie made her seat recline, bunched up a sweater against the window, and went to sleep.

Duff's mind wandered. In a vague aimless way, it drifted over the job question, it considered what his father might say when they next talked, it replayed the touch and the look in the restaurant several times, and eventually it settled on the puzzle of Stu and the money.

Stu had had the money in Albuquerque—he bought the Toyota with it and said there was a lot left over. It was almost certain that he'd had the money when he left the truck stop. So where had it been in between those two places? Where had it been when Rolf and Burl were looking for it?

Duff tackled this puzzle in his usual logical way, step by step.

Step 1: Stu finds the money in the Chevy at Rosalie Hopgood's house. He takes it. He has to put it either in his backpack or on his person—someone might find it if he hides it in the car.

Step 2: Location of money remains unchanged through Oklahoma City, Amarillo, and Sunlight Village. There would be no reason to move it.

Step 3: Chevy breaks down at remote gas station. If Stu *does* have the money hidden in the car (unlikely), he would certainly move it at this point.

Step 4: They arrive at Aunt Shirley's. Stu buys the Toyota, paying with cash. He puts the money in a new hiding place, not on himself, not in his backpack, not in any easy-to-find place in the car. Why would he do this? Why not keep carrying it wherever he'd had it before? Because Duff knew about it now, that's why. Stu didn't trust Duff any more than Duff trusted Stu.

Okay. So when, during the stay at Aunt Shirley's, did Stu have time to scurry around hiding money? He'd been within Duff's sight almost every minute—except for when he was out in Shirley's garage, checking over the Toyota. That had to be when he'd hidden the cash—the only time no one was with him.

Except Moony, of course, who was out there in his crate, banned from coming into the house.

And suddenly it all fell into place. "Got it!" Duff shouted.

Bonnie jolted awake. "What, what?" she said, sitting straight up, her eyes darting back and forth.

"We have to stop," said Duff. He slowed down and pulled over onto the side of the highway.

Bonnie grabbed the armrest. "What's the matter? Is the car breaking down?"

"No, no. I just figured something out." Duff got out of the car, opened the back door, and lifted out Moony's crate. He set it on the ground and opened its door. Holding on to Moony, he pulled the disgusting cushion out from under him. Bits of whitish fluff came with it, the result of Moony's scratchings.

"*What* are you doing?" Bonnie stood over him with her hands on her hips. No doubt she thought he'd gone crazy.

Duff turned the cushion around until he'd found the biggest rip in its cover. He stuck his hand inside. There was definitely a space in there, but nothing was in it. He hadn't really expected there would be, but still he was a little disappointed. His theory was correct, though—he was sure about that.

"This is where Stu hid the money," he said.

"Inside Moony's *cushion*?"

"Yep. My guess is he stuck it in there just before he went to ask Shirley if he could buy the Toyota. Then when she told him what she wanted for it, he went back and got that much. The rest he jammed as far in as he could and packed the stuffing around it."

"It wasn't that great a hiding place," Bonnie said. "Burl could have found it if he'd looked just a little bit harder."

"The barf helped a lot," said Duff. "That was a real piece of luck for Stu."

"And so, when we stopped at the truck stop, and Stu said he'd clean the cushion, he wasn't just being helpful."

"He was cleaning out the *inside* of the cushion," said Duff.

"So then," said Bonnie, sitting down on the backseat with her legs out the side of the car, "do you think he had this plan in mind the whole time? He never meant to keep the bargain he made with you?"

"I don't know." Duff felt inside the cushion one more time, just to make sure Stu hadn't left them even a little consolation prize, but he felt nothing but cotton fluff. "Maybe he meant it when he said it. But then here was this perfect opportunity—a place where trucks are heading south, where he can get a ride without standing out on the highway, where he can slip off to the men's room with a really good excuse to take the cushion with him—maybe it was all just too much to resist."

"Probably," said Bonnie. "Well, I can't be too upset about it. What would I have done with that money anyway? I'd have had to turn it in to the police. I'm just as glad not to have to deal with it." She sighed. "Too bad about the nonexistent friend in LA, though. I guess I was dumb to believe him about that."

They got back in the car. Moony rode on Bonnie's lap. She wrapped her arms around him and rested her chin lightly on his head.

Three hundred miles to go, Duff told himself.

Even though his back hurt from driving so long, and his plan for Stu and the money had failed, and his future loomed ahead of him like the shadowy gulf below a cliff, he was happy. It was a straight shot now—all he had to do was drive.

Chapter 19
SUNSET OVER THE OCEAN

You wouldn't think driving could make a person as tired as it does. After all, you're sitting down the whole time, and you're not doing anything very strenuous with your muscles, just pressing with your foot and moving your arms a little bit. But hour after hour of driving, the whole body in more or less one position, the hands gripping, the eyes looking always forward, the legs with not too many choices of where to go—it wears you out worse than running, or biking, or anything Duff had ever done before. It was even worse after it got dark, and there was nothing to look at except the taillights up ahead and the dotted line on the highway, endlessly zipping underneath the wheels of the car. Duff began to think of driving as something very much like torture.

Bonnie's voice kept him going. When they started getting closer to Los Angeles, and freeways curved and branched off from one another like a tangle of enormous concrete ribbons, she kept him from panicking. "Just follow the signs," she said. "Every time it says Santa Monica, go that way. That's all you have to do."

It seemed to Duff that the sound of tires on pavement was humming down deep in his bones, putting him into a trance. The whole daytime world had vanished, and all the thoughts that went with daytime were gone, too. His mind, usually such a yakker, was quiet and empty. Nothing existed except the darkness, the cars and trucks driving along with them, and the dotted white line.

Then he became aware of taillights flashing ahead.

People were putting on their brakes. Traffic was jamming up. "How could there be a traffic jam in the middle of the night?" he said.

"In Los Angeles," said Bonnie, "there can be a traffic jam anytime."

They slowed to a crawl. Sometimes they stopped completely, and an eerie silence came over everything. It was like being in a dream—the cars like strange humped creatures nosing forward, the shadowy figures inside them, the sense of being in a nowhere land, and not knowing why you were there, and being helpless to get out. They couldn't go forward, they couldn't go backward. They couldn't even escape by taking one of the exits off the freeway, because they'd end up lost in the vast maze of the city.

It didn't matter, though. They weren't in a hurry anymore. No job waited for Duff tomorrow morning. What difference did it make if they got to Amelia's by midnight or two AM or even seven in the morning?

So they crept forward inch by inch.

"What the world needs," said Duff after a long time, "is a car that flies."

"You could invent one," said Bonnie.

"Uh-huh," said Duff. They were too tired and spaced out even to carry on a conversation. The image of a flying car—a bubble-shaped thing with a couple of rockets for tailpipes—floated briefly through Duff's head. He pictured himself gunning the throttle and sailing up over the freeway, looking down from a distance at the long red necklace of taillights, and then zooming off into the sky, where no traffic jams could slow him down.

Finally, they came to the source of the problem: an enormous truck lying on its side, stretching across two full lanes and half of a third. Police cars and fire engines had nosed in around it like bugs around a carcass, their lights flashing. Flares spit white sparks. Fire had blackened the truck's cab. The seat was still smoldering, and a thin, throat-scorching smoke hovered in the air.

A scene from hell, Duff thought. Interesting that a traffic accident had marked both the beginning and the end of his cross-country journey. At least neither one had been *his* accident.

After that, traffic sped up again. Around two o'clock, having followed Bonnie's directions and gotten lost only a couple of times, Duff drove up in front of a small house and parked the car. The windows of the house were dark, but a porch light shone. When he opened the car door, he smelled the ocean, fresh and seaweedy. It was a new world.

"We made it!" shouted Bonnie. She sprang out of the car, slammed the door, and ran around to where Duff was standing zombielike at the curb. "You're a total *hero*!" she said, and she flung her arms around Duff and hugged him. The shock of this, plus the fact that exhaustion had dissolved his muscles, caused him to stagger backward, buckle at the knees, and collapse like a wet paper sack onto the ground.

Inside the house, a light went on.

• • •

"More orange juice?" said Amelia.

"Sure." Duff held out his glass.

He had slept last night on Amelia's couch and wakened to see morning light pouring through the windows. He'd glimpsed the back of a tall blond woman as she went out the front door—Linda, he learned later, off to her job as a hotel restaurant chef. Now, having taken his first shower in three days and dressed in the clothes he'd meant to wear on his first day of work, he was sitting on the deck outside Amelia's house, gazing at the endless ocean, where the morning sun was making the wavelets sparkle. Ernie, the bulldog, was snoring at his feet. Bonnie was swinging lazily in the hammock, half asleep, her arms around Moony, who was stretched out on top of her, his nose pressing against her chin.

Amelia sat down beside Duff. She was a slim, bright-eyed woman with brown hair cut straight across her forehead in bangs. "I understand you came out here for a job," she said.

"Correct," said Duff. "But now that I'm here, the job isn't."

"So I heard," said Amelia. She didn't say, "So what are you going to do now?" Duff appreciated that, since he wasn't sure of the answer. All he knew was that he was glad to be sitting here by the ocean, with a little space around him in which he could think about his next step.

Amelia and Bonnie went inside after a while and sat down across from each other at the kitchen table. Duff could tell from the way they settled in and their serious voices that they needed to have a good talk. So he fetched his laptop, took it out on the deck, plugged it in, and checked his e-mail. No apologies from Ping Crocker. Lots of spam. He went onto the Web and wandered around idly. Just for fun, he typed *a car that flies* into the search engine.

The results surprised him. It seemed that plenty of people were working on this concept. The guy who seemed the most serious was actually in California. He'd devoted his entire life to making a flying car that was guided by a very sophisticated computer program. According to his website, he was almost ready to launch. Incredible. It seemed like, all over the world, people hardly anyone had ever heard of were working on ideas that could change the whole course of the future. Why couldn't he be part of that somehow?

He sat there for quite a while, watching the seagulls diving and screaming, gazing out at the distant hazy line where the water met the sky. Thoughts of new possibilities swirled slowly around in his head, like ribbons of chocolate in vanilla ice cream. All this had started when the old Ford Escort broke down, and he'd stood at the window of the motel room in Chipper Crossing griping to himself about oil, something he'd hardly given a thought to in his entire previous life. Driving across the country had put the whole question of energy right in his face: What makes things go? Well, oil and gas. But not only those. Air could do it, too, and the sun, and french fry oil. Alternatives were out there; he'd just never noticed them before. But in the last five days, they'd been popping up everywhere. It was like when you hear a new word, one you've never heard even once—and then in the next week, you hear it five more times.

All that day, Duff thought and slept and walked on the beach with Bonnie. His mind churned sluggishly, trying to solve the problem of what to do next. But his usual logical powers had deserted him. Maybe they didn't work in the different air of California. Or maybe he was just tired.

At the end of the day, he and Bonnie sat once again on Amelia's deck, drinking lemonade made with lemons from Amelia's tree. The sun was setting spectacularly over the ocean, decorated with scarlet and violet and golden streamers of cloud. Duff gazed at this display.

"It's the smog that makes those colors," Bonnie said.

And at that, a vision arose before Duff's inner eyes. He saw the entire planet wrapped in a miles-thick woolly blanket of bad air, glowing an evil orange, gradually smothering all the little life-forms struggling beneath it. The picture was as clear in his mind as a really good computer animation.

Phone Call #8

Tuesday, July 2, 8:35 AM

Duff: Hi, Dad. I'm in California.

Duff's father: Great! You're calling from work?

Duff: Well, no. Things have sort of changed.

Duff's father: Changed how?

Duff: That job with Incredibility didn't work out.
I mean, the company tanked.

Duff's father (long pause): I see.

Duff: But I have a whole new angle on my career
now. The thing is, though, I'll probably have
to go to school. And I don't exactly have a
place to stay yet. Or a job, which I need right
away, because I more or less used up most of
my money. I don't actually have a car right
now, either.

Duff's father (after another long, dire pause): Two
words, Duff: Wade Belcher. Call him.

Duff: Well, but I thought maybe I'd like to stay
in Los Angeles, if you could just lend me—

Duff's father: Call him, Duff. Do it now. And
then call me back and explain how
you got yourself in this situation.

Duff: It's kind of a long story.

Duff's father: I will look forward to hearing it.
Talk to you soon, Son, when you and
Wade have a plan.

Chapter 20
A WHOLE DIFFERENT FUTURE

It turned out that Wade Belcher wasn't the boring old dinosaur Duff expected him to be after all, or at least he didn't sound like one over the phone. He talked fast, laughed often, and seemed sincerely glad to hear from his old friend's son. He told Duff that he was planning to rent out the top floor of his house, a refurbished Victorian in an old part of San Jose, near the university. But since the work on the place wasn't quite done yet—they were still putting in the new windows in the tower room—he'd let

Duff stay there a while for free as he looked for a job.

So Duff abandoned his vision of the apartment complex and the swimming pool, and he bought a plane ticket to San Jose. Bonnie and Amelia drove him to the airport. They dropped him off outside the terminal. Bonnie opened the trunk, and he hoisted out his duffel bag and his laptop. Before he'd had a chance to think about how to say good-bye, she flung her arms around him, nearly knocking him backward. "Bye," she said into his ear. "Come and see me when I get famous." Then she kissed him. On his mouth. It was not just a quick peck—it must have lasted three full seconds. Duff's duffel bag slid off his shoulder and thumped down at his feet. His whole being was bedazzled.

Bonnie jumped back in the car, waved out the window with Amelia waving behind her, and the car pulled away. Duff stood still and watched until he couldn't see it anymore. It took him a moment to get his legs working, but he made it through the airport and onto the plane. During the flight, he replayed that kiss several hundred times. It was wonderful every time. He felt new. His face, dimly reflected in the tinted airplane window, looked different to him—stronger along the jaw, and without the morose, guarded expression it used to have. He would grow his hair a little longer, he thought, and comb it sideways. He was tired of the furry-animal look. He wanted to look on the outside the way he felt now on the inside—not only like a man of intelligence, as he'd always been, but like a man of action, too, a bold and purposeful man, a man with heart.

Phone Call #9

Wednesday, July 3, 11:03 AM

Duff: Hello?

Stu: Hey, man, it's me.

Duff: Stu?

Stu: Yeah, your favorite traveling companion.

Where are you?

Duff: The San Jose airport—I just got off the plane.

Where are *you*?

Stu: The beach, man! Mexico.

Duff: *Mexico?*

Stu: Yeah. I needed to get away.

Duff: Right. You got away with a lot.

What happened to our deal?

Stu: Well, that's what I'm calling about. I've been

feeling a little bit bad.

Duff: A little bit?

Stu: So I'm sending some of that money back to

Bonnie, and I need her address.

Duff: Why not all of it?

Stu: Well, some of it's gone.

Duff: Gone where?

Stu: Here and there. Some I gave away to some folks
who looked like they needed it. Some I spent.

Duff: Bonnie's still at her aunt's. It's 2309 Veranda
Way, Santa Monica. [Pause.] How'd you
get my cell phone number?

Stu: It was on your business card.

Duff: I never gave you my card.

Stu: It was in your wallet.

Duff: Oh. [Pause.] Wait. My wallet?

Stu: Which I happened to cop off the counter
at Pete's Stewpot.

Duff: You? *You* stole my wallet?

Stu: Just temporarily, man. Don't get upset. I'll send
your money back, if you want.

Duff: You'd better.

Stu: I got a job, is the thing. I'll be making my
own money now. [Pause.] Don't you want
to know what it is?

Duff: Okay, what is it?

Stu: Driving a car for a rich American guy!

Duff: Great. Are you planning to rip him off, too?

Stu: No, no, man. I'm through with crime. It's the straight path for me. So listen—if you ever come down here, look me up.

Duff: How would I—and what about my—

Stu: See ya, man.

[Click.]

The Last Chapter and
THE LAST PHONE CALL

One day shortly after Duff had moved in to the tower room in Wade Belcher's house, as he was sitting by the window looking through the San Jose State University catalogue, his cell phone rang. He unhooked it from his belt. "Hello?"

"Hi," said a voice on the other end. "It's me."

Duff's heart jumped in his chest like a happy frog. *"Bonnie?"*

"Yeah. I have some news to tell you."

"Oh! Okay. Great!" With his free hand, he hoisted

the window open, and warm, jasmine-scented air flowed in. "What news?" he said.

"Two things. The first one is, I talked to my mom. She's still in the hospital. She is so *furious* about what happened! And on top of the whole thing about the money, Rolf and Burl got arrested!"

"They did? What for?"

"Because they threatened the guys at the gas station and pushed them around, and the guys called the police. And the police were really glad to get their hands on Rolf and Burl, because they were wanted for a whole lot of stuff. They're in jail now in Albuquerque."

Duff smiled. Bad guys lose, he thought, remembering Stu's triumphant whoop. "And what happened to the car?" he asked.

"Confiscated," said Bonnie. "It'll sit in a garage somewhere and wait till my mother comes to claim it. She'll sell it, I'm sure. And maybe she'll use the money to start herself on a better kind of life."

Duff leaned against the window frame, gazing out

over the rooftops of his new neighborhood. "Well, that's all really good," he said. "I mean, I guess your mom and Rolf and Burl don't think so, but it seems fair to me."

"Me, too," said Bonnie. "So here's the second piece of news. There's this place called the Bluebird Café. They've hired me for Friday nights, to sing."

"I told you so!" Duff said. "I knew you'd get discovered."

"And I made up a new song," said Bonnie. "It's called 'Brand-New Car.' It's kind of about you."

"About *me*? Really?"

"Uh-huh. Want to hear the last part of it?"

"Sure," said Duff. "Of course."

"Okay, stand back." He heard Bonnie take a deep breath, and then her great vibrant singing voice belted these words into his ear:

"You can't even know
Where he's going to go,
Or how far
In his new kind of car.

And he's on a new road,
A cool road,
A fast road,
He's on a new road now."

    Duff was speechless for a moment.

    "Do you like it?" Bonnie asked.

    "I do," said Duff. "I can't tell you how great I think it is." He stood gazing into the feathery leaves of the palm tree, his ears ringing, his mind blissfully empty, and his heart running like a little engine, fast and smooth.